PUFFS AND PACHYDERMS

STORIES FROM THE NILGIRIS AND ASSAM

R. PREMKUMAR

Illustrations by S. Shreeshail,
Art Teacher, JNV Chikkamagaluru

notionpress.com

INDIA • SINGAPORE • MALAYSIA

ISBN 979-8-89066-939-1

Dedicated to the memory of

my Dad, PV Rajan,

and my Mom, PJ Rachel,

who were my first readers.

Contents

Reader's Take on the Stories

"Mr. Prem Kumar wears many hats, in addition to being an able educator. His foray into writing has led to the curation of many thought-provoking and engaging pieces of content. His latest anthology, titled *Puffs and Pachyderms*, proves his mettle as a consummate writer capable of weaving great stories with their souls rooted in the beautiful countryside. I am convinced that readers would enjoy reading his latest anthology and derive a vicarious experience of traversing the sylvan surroundings of Nilgris & Northeast."

– Anabik Chakraborty, Calcutta

"I find myself being transported into a world filled with rich forms of imagery, ranging across the auditory, visual, and olfactory landscapes. I find within these stories a profound sense of nostalgia, which allows me to relate with every character, be it human or animal! I'm left wondering if I could be momentarily transported to the worlds created by such a deeply observant writer."

– Benjamin Eric George, Canada

"The stories draw upon the writer's experiences with the wild, the wilderness and explores the human–nature relationship. The writing is poetic, interspersed with pithy quotes about nature, human life and emotions. *Puffs and Pachyderms* takes you on a trail to the soul of the blue mountains of the Western Ghats and the heart of the Northeast through the tales of its inhabitants. The book is an ode to goodness, beauty and truth"

– Suresh, Chikkamagaluru

"R. Premkumar is a master storyteller, obliged by his profession to be exceptionally observant, much like his kindred elephant friends. This set of short stories is a window to the rich experiences of his life, the likes of which today cannot be afforded by dwellers of concrete jungles. His love of life and people sparkles throughout this book."

– Shirish Hirekodi, Bangalore

"*Puffs and Pachyderms* is a soulful narration of the author's experiences. His love for the majestic giants is reflected in anecdotes on pachyderms. His diction is as crisp as the layers in the puffs, and stuffed with a perfect blend of emotions, experience, and adventure. The reader gets gluttonous to devour the book."

– Geetha, Palaghat, Kerala

"With his words, the author makes mundane life special and ordinary people heroes. He has an eye for capturing nature like a seasoned lensman. He paints a lucid picture of things around us that most people fail to take note of. His narration is so captivating that one is compelled to read the stories in one go… and is left wanting for more! A master storyteller and a poet par excellence!"

– *Rajkumar Mane, Maharashtra*

"The adventures have been brought in front of my eyes. Beautifully penned. Love to read about the scenic Nilgiris, the beautiful friendship of besties in school, and the carefree days of childhood. Love it."

– *Ms Sumita Devi, Muscat*

"Mr. Premkumar's work embarks on a journey of self-discovery with insightful observations of the diversity of nature, people, and all living things. His exquisite writings cover a large repertory of characters from real life that are a transcendent experience for the readers."

– *Palanivelu, North & Middle Andamans*

"Mr. Premkumar's writings have always kept me enthralled… they are so real, so lively... He writes what he feels and his storytelling has often captivated me for a whole day. He possesses a unique ability to grip his readers' feelings."

– *Sushravya Jeevala, Hassan*

"In this remarkable short story compilation, readers embark on a captivating and nostalgic journey through the author's life, awed by his exceptional ability to recall vivid details and his discerning eye for observation. The author's profound sensitivity and perceptive nature shine through, as he seamlessly weaves together vibrant descriptions, poignant emotions, and engaging plotlines. With universal appeal rooted in relatable experiences, these thought-provoking stories prompt introspection, evoking a shared sense of nostalgia and leaving an indelible imprint on the hearts and minds of readers."

– Jemuel Stanley, USA

"The stories of Mr. Premkumar are realistic and air-dashes me to my childhood days in the mesmerizing Nilgiris. I resonate with every minute aspect of the stories, be it a leaf, a bird or a flower. As a master storyteller, the author dextrously makes it alive and sensational even after decades."

– Sukanya, USA

"The thrill of his nostalgic childhood adventures & vast travel experiences is transferred to the reader. His stories are filled with awe and suspense. A fantastic narration of animals in general and pachyderms in particular."

– Jaybharathi, Mysore

"The narrations are incredibly powerful and the characters are portrayed so realistically that it connects us on an emotional level with long-lasting impact. A truly touching and unforgettable reading experience."

– Abina, Kerala

"These set of stories are touching, gripping and is consumed in a go… Loved reading them for their plot and presentation. The attractive diction is informative, interesting, educative and entertaining."

– Ms Vanashree, Mangalore

"Exceptional writer with his texts brimming with emotions."

– Uma Burman, Assam

"*Puffs and Pachyderms* is a collection of heart-warming and humorous stories that will leave you feeling good. The characters are well-developed and relatable, and the plots are engaging and unpredictable. The writing is clear and concise, and the stories are full of vivid imagery."

– Sister Jecintha Shanthi Desa AC, Mangalore

Also by R Premkumar:

Love Beyond (2019) – An Anthology of 104 Poems

with illustrations by NA Patel, Art Teacher JNV Shimoga

Foreword

Mr. A N Ramachandra
Former Joint Commissioner with NVS,
Ministry of Education, Govt. of India.

I have immense pleasure to introduce this anthology of stories from a nature-loving teacher and a passionate storyteller. Being a person born and brought up in remote villages, I get this rare opportunity to reflect upon the transformative power of nature and its profound impact on our lives through this anthology. I am reminded of the guidance of John Muir, who once said, *"In every walk with nature, one receives far more than he seeks."* I personally feel that nature has a remarkable ability to nurture our souls, awaken our senses, and guide us towards a deeper understanding of ourselves and the society we are associated with.

Having lived in many cities across India in the last forty years and having endured a fast-paced society, I myself felt disconnected from the natural world that sustains us. Amidst the hum of machines, constant demands of social lives, and chaotic backdrop, our villages and forests patiently waited for my return, ready to offer solace, wisdom, and a profound sense of belonging.

This anthology brings together a collection of fifteen stories from Shri R Premkumar, a humble teacher, who has devoted his entire life to cultivating a deep and intimate relationship with nature and upholding the values in Human Life. Through '*Uncle Captain*' Prem suggests that we learn lessons from everyone. Through these stories, we embark on a journey that transcends the boundaries of our daily routines and transports us to the enchanting realm of forests, rivers, mountains, and meadows. We encounter the untamed beauty of wildlife, especially the awe-inspiring power of Tuskers, and the delicate balance that exists within ecosystems. Most of the stories recollect his childhood in the hills of Nilgiris where he was raised and to the plains of Assam, where he embarked on an official stint. His bond with his father, grandparents, friends, and teachers is succinctly explored.

The author makes a genuine choice of diction in his narratives. In '*The Anklet Dreamer,*' Swapna's desire to have a silver anklet leads the reader to think vividly about the types of desires we need to host and push through. Delicate details indicate the required wisdom in the choice of desires in life and the required direction in dreams. The subject matter of '*Brahmaputra Mail*' being unconditional love, explains the fabric of parental love for the kids. The sequences unfolded in the story bring out the theme of faith in human responses. The details unfolded in the '*Brahmaputra Mail*' also show how a motherly feeling attracts the entire world. Beyond being an author, Prem has stepped out to understand the life of mahouts and spent energy in honouring them, for bringing the gentle giants nearer to human life at the risk of their personal life.

As you delve into these tales, you will find yourself amidst the rustling leaves of ancient trees, listening to the melodious songs of birds, and feeling the gentle caress of a breeze on your skin. You will witness the resilience and adaptability of the natural world, as well as the intricate interconnectedness that binds every living organism, including wildlife. The stories are not just restricted to permeating nostalgia but give messages to the practising teachers on organizing experiences for the learners.

Beyond the captivating narratives lies a deeper message, one that resonates with the core of our being. It is a message that speaks of the need to nurture our relationship with nature, to cherish and protect the fragile ecosystems that sustain life on our planet. These stories will illuminate the harmonious symphony of plants and animals and the profound lessons that nature holds for us. The message in Bajji's return does not stop at the joy of finding the friend back in life, but the caution one needs in the diverse life, cohabitation, and coexistence. As an educationist, Prem repeatedly calls the readers to raise the bar of affectionate facilitation in teaching, modernizing the style of education through clear guidance to take the students to nature and make them learn with empathy. Nine of the fifteen stories in this anthology are around the childhood life of the author, who is deeply influenced by pachyderms. He vividly remembers his first encounter with elephants as a school-going child, during a film shooting in his school campus. There is an element of the supernatural in '*The Girl With the Pitcher*,' '*Behold What Manner of Love*' and '*Ghost in the Walnut Tree*.' '*Farooq's Goat*' is a direct call to educational administrators to host therapy pets in schools. National Pride bubbles in many stories.

These stories are not only the subject of rejoicing for the author but also a feast for the readers to learn from nature. Through these stories, our nature-loving teacher imparts the wisdom gained from years of observation, contemplation, and reverence for the natural world. They remind us of the importance of preserving biodiversity, practising sustainable living, and cultivating a sense of stewardship towards our environment. Flow in the narration sustains the interest of the readers till the end. The sudden twist in a few stories is enthralling. '*Uncle Captain*' can never be taken out of his mind.

I hope this anthology will take you beyond and inspire you to reconnect with nature, embark on your own journey of discovery, and heed the whispers that emanate from the wilderness to work for its rich values. Prem's life is profoundly influenced by the versatile support of nature for human life, and more so by the majestic presence of elephants. This impacts not only Prem but also his readers, including his family, who get attuned to a deep admiration for nature through his writings.

Allow the tales to awaken the desire to reconnect with nature, and uphold the values in education. As you turn the pages, I am sure you will find a renewed commitment to embrace nature's whispers in your own life.

– A N Ramachandra

Mr. S V Seshadri
Founder Principal JNV Belgaum
Former Asst. Director NVS RO Hyderabad
HRD Ministry, Govt. of India

"*I have spent a fortune travelling to distant shores and looked at lofty mountains and boundless oceans, and yet I haven't found time to take a few steps from my house to look at a single dewdrop on a single blade of grass.*"

– *Rabindranath Tagore*

Gurudev regretted not having taken that time to appreciate the beauty of nature in little things. Prem on the other hand has appreciated and enjoyed the tiniest of pleasures that nature has to offer. His postings in various Navodaya Vidyalayas all over the country have given him a fertile opportunity to embrace the arms of Mother Nature.

Having been born and brought up in the pristine Nilgiri Hills, surrounded by evergreen forests with beautiful fauna and flora, Premkumar befriended the forest and its inmates. From the rhinos of Kaziranga to lions of the Gir, elephants of Sakrebyle to the birds of Mandagadde, a reflection of this can be seen in '*Call from the Wild*'; from betel nuts of Shivamogga to the aromas of coffee beans from Chikkamagaluru, one can even get a glimpse of the supernatural element in '*Ghost in the Walnut Tree*'; every animal, from humans to insects have tickled his creative nerve, '*The Girl with the Pitcher*' is one such story. As an educationist and a good administrator, his keen interest in the overall well-being of his students can be seen in his suggestion to introduce therapy pets in school. A peek into such initiative is seen in '*Farooq's Goat.*' Even inanimate things like streams, dew drops, and rain… he has an eye for each of them.

His writings help us visualize and he truly paints a picture with words. He has the capability of keeping his readers hooked to his works!

Like Robert Frost said,

> "*The woods are lovely, dark and deep,*
> *But I have promises to keep,*
> *And miles to go before I sleep,*
> *And miles to go before I sleep.*"

For you Prem, I would say:

> "*The nature is lovely, bright and beautiful,*
> *Many more colours of hers to be unearthed,*
> *Pray your eyes are always fervent and hopeful*
> *To pen these colours that are always delightful.*"

This anthology of short stories – *Puffs and Pachyderms* – has a wide range of genres that will surely satiate every reader's interest. Here's wishing you a very happy writing, Prem.

– S V Seshadri

Note From a Young Author

Immerse yourself in the captivating world of *Puffs & Pachyderms*, where the mundane day-in-day-out cycle is left far behind. With each tale, Mr. Premkumar skilfully weaves together a tapestry of emotions, transporting you to a vibrant and diverse universe.

Drawing inspiration from personal experiences and heartfelt conversations with individuals from all walks of life, the stories resonate with the universal essence of the human spirit. From the depths of adventure to the heights of love, friendship, inspiration, and mysticism, there is a tale waiting to unfold for every mood and inclination.

With profound eloquence, Mr. Premkumar captures the essence of life's profound moments—the ebbs and flows of joy, the weight of grief, the resilience in times of challenge, and the power of unity and solidarity. These stories remind us that, at our core, we are all connected by a shared humanity, regardless of our affluence, backgrounds, education, or beliefs.

Prepare to be captivated by the sheer brilliance of Mr. Premkumar's storytelling. His narratives will stir your soul, leaving you with a renewed sense of empathy and a deeper understanding of the human experience. Through his words, you will venture beyond your own boundaries and partake in the extraordinary.

So, dive in, turn the pages, and let these stories transport you to a world brimming with life's infinite possibilities.

– Tanya Sharon

Chennai.

"I felt my lungs inflate with the onrush of scenery – air, mountains, trees, people. I thought, 'this is what it is to be happy.'"

– Sylvia Plath

Preface

In standard four, I scripted my maiden story and the first readers were my parents. They were jubilant that their child attempted something original and creative. That story was thrust upon an aunt who read it reluctantly and eventually exclaimed, "Considering his age, it is good." During high school, I rolled out a couple of anecdotes, snippets, and stories that were well-received by my peers.

My grandma was a good raconteur. As a child, I was absorbed by her stories. Her stories predominantly had an element of the supernatural. She kept us in good humour with old family stories, her childhood adventures in Kotagiri, and particularly of Nicholson, her mischievous cousin. She recounted numerous elephant stories that are still etched in my mind. Listening to the near-death experiences was jittery. Grandma was a chronic dreamer as well and they flowed typically like a story.

I have tried reconstructing some of her stories, and still have many in the waiting. During my teaching career, beginning in the early 90s, these stories came alive in the classrooms and

I followed the story-based pedagogy, which is much harped about today.

I have always been a votary of short stories for its brevity, easy reading, a facile flow, and sometimes a twist at the end.

Puffs and Pachyderms comprises fifteen short stories. Several of them are memoirs of my childhood in the Nilgiris written during the COVID period. The themes range across juvenile adventure, friendship, infatuation, fancies, tributes, and musings of nature that are canopied in all the stories. My experiences with the elephants are reflected in '*The Call from the Wild*.' A few stories have overtones of the supernatural. '*Anklet Dreamer*,' '*In Brahmaputra Mail*,' and '*Farooq's Goat*' are stories based in Assam. '*Anklet Dreamer*' depicts the life of an abysmally poor Assamese family and features Swapna, a young girl, and her mom Jonali. '*In Brahmaputra Mail*' is a train journey that binds the travellers together, exemplifying the spirit of Indianness, despite the diversities. '*Farooq's Goat*' is depicted as a therapy pet that makes a difference in the life of children in a boarding school. '*I Can't Stop Loving You*' is essentially a passionate love story of Uncle William, a septuagenarian. '*Uncle Captain*' is about a stranger that I met as a child.

The special bond that I enjoyed with my dear grandpa, my extraordinary high-school teacher, and a cherished friend is also showcased within the pages of this anthology.

In the first place, these stories are a gift unto myself. They are close to my heart. Reminiscing and recreating them is like reliving those moments afresh once again. The writing experience is a celebration, one of thanksgiving and catharsis.

To me life is not a matter of just milestones, but intoxicating moments that are ephemeral. I value the beauty of each fleeting moment and have endeavoured to preserve them in these stories.

I thank my friends and readers who have delighted in my writings. May I invite the readers to join me on the journey to those golden moments that I cherish in my heart always.

– R Premkumar

prembenayah@gmail.com

Acknowledgements

I profusely express my gratitude to Mr. Ashok Kumar Sharma, PGT Computer Science JNV Shimoga, who typed the major portion of stories during the COVID period. I thank my eldest son Samuel Wesley for his extraordinary insight & patience in editing all these fifteen stories, and for designing the cover page as envisioned. Without his support, this anthology wouldn't have been feasible to publish. I also extend my appreciation to Mr. Shreeshail, Art Teacher JNV Chikamagaluru, for his apt illustrations that beautifully complement my stories.

I express my gratitude to Mr. AN Ramachandra, former Joint Commissioner NVS, for his insightful Foreword and for conceiving the idea for the cover page of *Puffs and Pachyderms*.

I also profusely thank Shri SV Seshadri, former Assistant Director of NVS RO Hyderabad, for taking the time to write the Foreword and for zealously engaging with my writings.

I thank my best friend for supporting me in this venture.

I am indebted to Notion Press for the professional help and platform to showcase my writings.

"Childhood is the one story that stands by itself in every soul."

– Ivan Doig

When the Robin Had Hopped

Jasmine was my childhood chum when we were about six or seven years old. We had studied together in 'Breeks', an Anglo-Indian school in the Nilgiris which was five kilometres away from the Hindustan Photo Films Township, where we had resided. Our parents had worked in H.P.F., which produced the iconic photo films of yesteryears and was once the 'golden goose' of the Nilgiris. It had lost its foothold in the market until it was declared a sick unit. But in our times, the company had commanded a monopoly in film manufacturing, and the H.P.F. company and premises were always bustling.

I had daily boarded the school bus from the first terminus, near the main gate of the factory. The bus spun around the township to pick up the kids. Jasmine had waited in the third terminus. I would await her presence each day. It was my duty to reserve her seat beside me. Her preferences swayed between the window and the aisle. I gladly yielded to her choices. As a child, I felt it my unwritten responsibility to make Jasmine comfortable. My fondness for her, I thought, surpassed hers for me. I felt a sense of comfort, belongingness in having her warmth. We would exchange chocolates, cakes, and pleasantries or sometimes I was lucky to be gifted with a tiffin box, a fragrant rose, a small Dahlia, a Chrysanthemum, or the indigenous wild berries ('*Thavittu Palam*', '*Vikki Palam*' etc.) of the Nilgiris. More than the gifts she had bestowed, I was enamoured by her bubbly presence.

Jasmine was wheatish, her cheeks were chubby; her eyes were like a dove's. Her cute dimple made her smile beauteous. Like a little Robin, she had hopped into the bus each day, and I followed her chirpy movements.

She had numerous things to recount each day. She prattled, all the way, while I sat glued, giving my full audience to her. She had occupied the best portion of the seat. All four years we had huddled to school together, and she had kept my school trips lively. I dreamt, each night to spin off swiftly to make an eternity of the twenty minutes beside her cherubic presence in the morn and the evening.

She was a born narrator and she had blown me away with her absorbing stories. I hardly remember what I had learnt at school, but I can still walk blindfolded through her stories. She was an inspiring little teacher. Her eyes dilated like a glittering marble when she was lost in her narratives. Her alluring dimple often distracted me from falling in rhythm with the ecstatic torrent of stories and their tapestries. Even the mundane things were woven as an appealing story in her own sprightly style. While she brought her rich collection of dolls to show me, in reciprocation, I stealthily carried my toys; scarce though.

In this, I rejoiced that I had little Jasmine all to myself for the twenty minutes in the morn and evening every day. But during the day in school, we hardly took notice of each other. I saw her sometimes flitting like a butterfly spreading her hues on the school premises.

The stories of Jasmine were funny and also had a supernatural element to it. She was nicknamed a 'chatterbox' and that's what she was. I was tolerant of her dominance, and my timidity sought refuge in it.

One of her unforgettable dreams still lingers with me. A giant walks into her room at midnight and kidnaps her by bringing a spell of slumber upon her family. While she screamed, her voice was choked. The giant gently carried her into the night, trod across the hillock, crossed the lake with ease, and hurtled through the deep woods.

Beyond the hills, there was another lake to be crossed, but the distance and height and depths, he licked it away with the gargantuan strides and leaps. Little Jasmine shut her eyes and was crouching in fear, but the Giant spoke kindly. He said,

"Daughter, be of good cheer, I promise you, I will not harm you. You are a rare gem."

Jasmine would plead, "Giant Uncle, please take me back home; my mom and dad would be worried."

Then from the deep valley, he walked into the thick woods and crossed the thorny bushes and rocks. A prowling leopard in the dark shirked in fear and gave way to the giant. The foxes ceased their frightening howls and receded. The boars retreated and grunted in terror.

Deep inside the jungle, the giant rolled back a rock over the mouth of a cave, which was hardly noticeable due to the dense vegetation and undergrowth. Jasmine was peering into the stillness, with her half-open eyes. She thought she must be now inside a den. Again, the giant reached out in the most amiable and gentlest way. "Don't worry, little one, you are in for a surprise." As they advanced into the cave, the long winding road led them onward to another salubrious world, looming large. In a little distance, there was a palatial building, the kind of which she had never seen.

A sprawling garden and orchards abounded with a plethora of exotic flowers and birds, surrounding the palace. Rabbits, turtles, and deer were hopping and playing in merriment. A magnificent band had welcomed her and ushered her into the palace. A host of courtiers were now attending to her. After a quick shower, she was arrayed with royal garments. Jasmine had described her attire to the minutest detail. She was small but mature beyond her age. Her communication, her understanding, and her insight were phenomenal.

The humble schoolgirl was magically transformed into a princess in no time. She was ushered into the presence of the king and queen. They were gracious to her and their words and gestures were endearing. She was bestowed with all the bounties and she was soon basking in splendour and glory.

At this juncture, Jasmine paused, looked into my eyes, and said, "Prem, would you like to accompany me to that land of splendour and glory." I recall telling her, "I would like to certainly visit, but not remain there."

Jasmine had narrated this dream for one whole week, in crunchy slices and presented before me like a seasoned chef. She was a prolific storyteller.

I wonder how many such stories I would have savoured for the first four years during my pre-primary days.

During the vacations after standard four, I was counting the days for the school to reopen. I had missed her for the full two months. I was ready earlier than usual. I vividly remember the red and grey Ashok Leyland bus trudging through the H.P.F. township. The bus passed by the sylvan surroundings with the towering eucalyptus trees in the Sholas, the placid lake lying like a huge python, the temple and the church on the hillock, the stream crackling beneath the pine forest, and the cluster of quarters.

As the bus halted at the next terminus, my eyes were frantically searching for my little Jasmine. Every single child was there except her. That was the first disappointment, perhaps, I had experienced as a child as far as I remember. I could not reconcile with the vacant seat that day and the absence of Jasmine, who had become a part of my life by now.

That evening, I sobbed and told Mom, "I would not be going to school as Jasmine wasn't coming." Seeing me sulking and turning rebellious, my mom had enquired to find that Jasmine was admitted to the Nazareth Convent, a school exclusively for girls.

Blatantly my mom declared, "Son, she will not come with you henceforth." Sadly, I never met Jasmine after that, although news regarding her whereabouts kept trickling.

Years upon years sped.

One day, I was in the hills for vacation. I took my customary stroll in the evening to my favourite scenic spots. There was a drizzle, and the air was thick with a eucalyptus tinge. I saw a jubilant couple in the distance sauntering towards me. I guessed I saw a familiar face; on second look, I confirmed that it was Jasmine. She must have been in her early twenties and evidently newly-wed. She was clinging on to her husband. Clad in a saree, she looked gorgeous.

The child in me naturally craved to yell out and run towards her. I wanted to clasp her fingers. But my education and my age restrained me. I began to reason out, what if she doesn't recognize me? What if she gets embarrassed? How would her husband react?

The equation changes with a woman, especially in India, the moment she gets married. I decided to avoid interrupting her. I blessed her and let go of the opportunity. But I was overwhelmed with the same childlike feelings.

In a twinkling of an eye, I was transported to the morns of my Breeks days. She dazzled before me with her pleated black skirt and black blazer, and a tie with black and red stripes. The sensation of her fingers crushing me, and my little fingers gently feeling her cute dimple played in my mind. The yellow and red umbrella had fluttered in the rain, with two kids hustling under its shelter.

Now, it's again years upon years since I last saw her gliding by. I only know for certain that in those four innocent years in Breeks, my little Jasmine was mine.

"Sometimes my childhood memories
sneak out of my eyes
and roll down my cheeks."

– Willow Teagan

Ghost in my Walnut Tree

The frantic thumping on the door of my home was frightening. The eerie darkness of that night exacerbated the silence.

Will the door succumb to it?

A kerosene lamp had flickered in the room. The brown carpet was faded and frayed. The furniture was scarce. A Philips radio covered in a red satin cloth was placed on the table.

I was there, a small weedy child pedalling my white and blue tricycle, clad in a high-necked, multi-coloured sweater, and muffled with a monkey cap.

The heavy downpour had just ceased, leaving puddles of water everywhere. The air was damp but was scented with eucalyptus and cypress.

The power was off. Perhaps somewhere a tree had fallen on the electric line. It's common to have power breakdowns during the monsoon in the hills. Mum was cooking and Dad hadn't returned home. The two of us were alone. The 'ding-dong' of the clock, flaunted on the wall, must have scared the rabbits. The clock had struck nine. "He must be coming on the last bus," muttered Mum.

My house lay beneath the Ooty-Mysore highway in a forty-acre field. The field had burst like a battalion in front of my home on all sides.

Ours was the first home in the fields that had sloped downwards. In the terraces, English vegetables, like potato, carrot, turnip, radish, cauliflower, and cabbage thrived.

A small gate with a few slippery steps on a descent led to our home. Honey flowers in purple and white abounded on the sides of the steps. I was the lucky 'bumble bee' to whom the blooms had yielded their nectar, obsequiously.

Five families had dwelt here in different corners. Our immediate neighbours were Jaya Aunty and her family. They were about half a kilometre from our home. Jaya Aunty, slightly squinted, was slim and tall, with an oval-shaped countenance. She had called me 'Bose', dragging the *ee* sound. The biblical

Boaz had corrupted into Bengali 'Bose'. Till the end, she stuck to it. "Bose... *Nalla Irukiya...ya.*" (Bose... How are you?)

Her turbaned father went shopping in the petty shops, with a faded grey coat and dhoti. Patti, Jaya Aunty's mum, had always offered me Nilgiri tea with *Ooty Varkey,* which I relished. Adept in traditional Tamil cuisine, her dishes were delightfully piquant. I was often left under their care.

Jaya Aunty and Mum were friends and had worked together in the Indu Film Factory, which manufactured photo films and X-rays.

Right in the middle of the fields, Mr. Abbas Bhai, the crafty, wily man had lived. He had many fair daughters followed by the curly-haired Sheriff.

The Ammitiyas – who were the landlords – lived in a farmhouse. Attired in his crumpled white shirt and pyjama pants, Mr. Ammitiya had his perfunctory stroll through his fields.

Asma, his eldest daughter was my nursery and primary school classmate. She had bobbed hair and was a frequent truant at the school. Despite Mrs Sampson's slaps, Maths continued to flummox me. I had dragged myself to school and showed no courage to join Asma, tempted though! Ironically, Asma works as a teacher in the same school now.

Syed and his family lived parallel to our home, but at the edge of the fields. They were absorbed in a permanent stint of altering their home.

A rivulet had crackled in the steep below Syed's house. A few pear trees were found near the rivulet. Beyond the rivulet, the Shola forests arose and expanded.

The dense, green, salubrious fields and Sholas greeted me each day.

As a child, I fancied all kinds of creatures and supernatural beings inhabiting and prowling deep in the Shola forests. Oh! How I had wished to adventure into the Sholas and the hills.

My home was tiled and was a simple, typical hill home with a slanted roof. The house must have been there for several years. There were huge eucalyptus trees and cypress trees behind.

In between the gate and behind our home, there stood an elegant walnut tree. Most of my early childhood memories are woven around it, my dumb but delightful companion.

walnut trees are considered to be a symbol of wisdom. But I had grown under it being ignorant of this belief. I had admired its height, its width, and its capacity to bear bounding walnuts. It had sheltered crows, mynahs, sparrows, and other birds. It prodded my inquisitiveness. I had nurtured it each day with a glass of water and it had thrived well. I had innocently ascribed its productivity, with its high nutritional-value fruit to my glass of water, which was poured forth with love each day.

During the summer, my walnut tree had shimmered with its smooth silver-grey bark and bright green, feathery leaves. In the monsoon, it had an astounding way of falling in tune with the boisterous winds and the ravaging rains. The winters were harsh and fierce. Sometimes, the temperature went dripping abysmally low in the Nilgiris. The frost had painted the grasslands, white. But my walnut tree showed remarkable aplomb. It stood there like a bastion. I was awed by its resilience.

Although I had sneaked to get near my walnut tree, my tonsillitis had played the villain and betrayed me. The only panacea was injections, flung like arrows by sister Hema on my bottoms, and the massage sessions that followed.

A white and brown country dog, which we called 'Kutty' rested under the walnut tree in the afternoons. A few crows joined her without any stir.

An old beggar with a stick and a bowl was also a coterie to the walnut tree. He slurped up his food noisily under its shade. His hungry eyes and the dented bowl haunt me even today. He had wheedled stories of his times, whenever he had the mood.

I rode my tricycle to my heart's desire under the wide spreading canopy of the walnut tree. I felt at home under its patronage. During vacations, Manju and Mala, nieces of Jaya Aunty, along with Asma had joined to play.

We picked the fallen fruits and also had pelted stones to pull down the walnuts.

Collectively, we sat to peel the fleshy green drupe and cracked corrugated woody shell with stones, which protects the nut's kernel. Sometimes we hurt our fingers while cracking the nuts. We relished the nuts, rich in vitamins and minerals.

I dreamt of a day when I would mount the tree and have an aerial survey of my home and the fields. I had dreamt of it parachuting me above the fields, across the rivulet, beyond the Sholas and hills and up in the azure sky. It was my magic wand.

Harvesting time was fun. Carrots and turnips were heaped in mounds. The shape, the colour, the texture, the taste was delectable, which I have never tasted ever after.

We played cookery using coconut shells. The mud paste assuming the shape of a coconut excited us and coaxed us to churn out idli, vada, pongal, upma, and a host of other dishes. The girls competed to serve me on the wild leaves as substitutes for banana leaves. Our hands-on training in cuisine, besides offering us experiential learning, also had cracked our tender skins, but that didn't deter our play.

My dad had organized my birthday celebration under the canopy of the walnut tree. All the families were invited. There was camaraderie in the small but heterogeneous community of ours. I grew up savouring the best of biriyani during Id and Ramzan, sweets on Diwali, and delicacies during Christmas.

The birthday song sounded more like a clangour, with its anglicized version of Tamil and Urdu, rendered in dissonance, with each one pitching differently. But that mattered little to me, as long as I was the little prince of the day.

One day, the beggar spilt beans into my mind that a ghost lives up there in my walnut tree in the night. I was petrified. I had imagined distorted visuals of the ghost. My discombobulated mind heard its heavy footsteps in the dark. I conjured diabolic and gory pictures of the ghost, shaking up the walnut tree with its fiery eyes and thorny fists. The child in me fancied the ghost making cheeky faces at me. Day and night, I was obsessive and too delicate to fixate on the ghost.

Now I began to connect the dots. No wonder folks stayed within after 7 pm and that's why my parents had forbidden me from playing near the walnut tree.

'Will it destroy my walnut tree? Is there no way to outwit the marauder and ferret it out? What if I own a magical gun to blow up the ghost into bits.' There was no end to my far-fetched frenzy and imagination.

However, the walnut tree was a thing of mystery to me. Although the ghost flounced about in our fields and near our home, the community was floundering to find a solution.

During one weekend, my parents suddenly decided to take me to my grandparents' home in Doddabetta. I always enjoyed being there, but this time I was too reluctant. Before we left, I made a clandestine visit to my walnut tree and half-clasped it. The feeling that surged through after the maiden hug was sensational. Nursing my tears, I feigned bravado before my parents.

I was grumpy and sulking in my grandparents' home. I had a nightmare that my walnut tree was abducted by the ghost. My uncle and aunts had conspired several baits to appease me. I had waited for my parents to take me back.

But it started raining heavily. The radio news said that the Nilgiris were reeling under a severe spell of floods. The villages and towns were flooded. Many houses were washed away. Many lost their lives.

Dad and Mom came after ten days. But they had different news for me. The floods had uprooted many trees and one of them fell on our home and damaged it. They thought it a wise and opportune time to relocate, and in my absence, they had shifted.

Life in my new home was unlike that in my previous home. It was closer to the factory. It was beside the highway. I've often seen folks alighting with huge bunches of coconuts from the Mysore bus.

A part of my precious childhood was severed. The walnut tree was still a bubble of romance to me.

I had desperately waited to watch the walnut tree from the school bus in the morning. Whenever Mom visited Jaya Aunty, I readily accompanied her.

I clasped my hand around the walnut tree. Earlier my clasps were too small, but as my visits became few and rare, my claps became bigger.

As I grew older, whenever I walked past the way, I could not but yield to the charms of my childhood chum. For years this pattern had persisted.

In the 90s I left the Nilgiris for Chennai to pursue my higher education. Life in the hills is cosy and intoxicating but my future was beckoning me. My college had widened my horizons. I became busy with the discovery and re-discovery of my career. Through these years, the verdant hills had always welcomed me with outstretched arms. I had never missed the sanctum sanctorum of my favourite spots.

This particular year, a rude shock awaited me. The fields, the Sholas, the rivulet had vanished. The place once teeming with natural vegetation and greenery had the resemblance of a young lady, who had tonsured her glistening hair that fell like a cascade.

It was heart-wrenching to notice the conspicuous absence of my walnut tree. It was callously uprooted with no remnants left.

The fields were converted into plots and sold in the guise of development. Mr. Ammitiya was lured by big offers. There was a huge influx from the villages to the town in search of jobs in H.P.F., their dream company. Brick and mortar now reigned supreme. A sea of humanity now jostle there, with hundreds of houses mushroomed.

I stood there mute and numb, envisioning the past and juxtaposing it with the present.

That strip of greenery might be only a tiny dot on the earth, but the earth ever since is surely lesser rich, lesser green, and lesser safe. That portion of my glorious world was sliced off. I wonder, how many such golden dots are wantonly sliced away. Who and what will atone for this heinous crime?

Life had moved on.

However, the walnut tree stayed with me, all the way. It had dazzled in my memory and had haunted my dream. One day, a nightmare disturbed me and set me on another pursuit.

The walnut tree lay floating in a pool of blood… The stars and heavenly bodies in unison were yelling out… Murder… Murder… Murder… The cry had thundered across the continents, mountains, and oceans. Tens and thousands of crows, mynahs, sparrows, eagles, and other creatures big and small had congregated to mourn its death. Mother Earth, stripped of her glory, raised her voice and wailed, mourning the loss of her progeny.

With all the seniors gone from the community, I had banked upon Sheriff and Syed to give me clues about the 'murder'.

The Hindustan Photo Films, once the pride of Nilgiris, was now declared as a sick unit. Mismanagement, complacency, and lack of vision led to the ruin. It lay like a colossal monster in paralysis. The employees were asked to leave. The future of thousands of families was at stake.

After my phone calls, discussions, investigations, and follow-up, I eventually zeroed in on Asma. She has been living there all the while, I was told.

"Hello Asma, this is Prem, calling you," from Assam.

"Which Prem?" she responded.

"Asma, I'm your nursery classmate and your playmate."

Again… silence. Perhaps her mind was racing back to the years and months that had fallen back…

"Hello, Prem," with no surprise, her voice sounded cold. I was at least glad, she figured me out… After the few exchanges, I came straight to the point, "What had happened to the walnut tree, Asma."

"Which walnut tree?" she again paused, hesitated, and gave me a flippant answer. Instead, she had invited me to her home. I hadn't seen Asma for almost four decades.

During my next trip to the Nilgiris, I had scheduled a meeting with Asma, as a top priority.

Asma had welcomed her playmate with her hand half stretched out. While I had shown excitement to meet my childhood playmate, she remained cold and passive. She also seemed to be lost in thoughts.

In her, I saw my own reflection.

In her, I saw my own present.

In her, I saw the flight of time.

In her, I saw the plight of life!

A new structure stood in the very place of their old home. Her house was furnished with the best of ornate work and stately furniture. As I was exchanging notes with her, nibbling the dry fruits and nuts, an object placed in the showcase caught my attention. It was an immaculate, black-and-white picture of her dad leaning against my walnut tree. I ran up to have a better view. It was magnificently framed with the finest of wood and put up there. I suppressed and swallowed my feelings, and smiled.

I asked her gently, "Asma tell me now, what happened to the walnut tree?" She heaved a sigh and pointed to the elegant furniture, sparkling wooden floor, and the imposing photo frame in the showcase while I stood in shock. She quipped,

"Prem, my father had bequeathed the walnut tree in memory of my grandfather." He had planted it when they had first lived there.

Now the stark truth of the demon who had chopped down "my walnut tree" came to light.

I felt sacrilegious to stand there. The gleam that had surrounded her house had suddenly turned sombre. I stood in silence as one who would mourn the loss of one's beloved in a sepulchre.

That was the first and the last time I had visited Asma.

The blows on the door felt like a thud. Mom stormed in with anxiety from the kitchen. With brazen courage, she unbolted the door. The door had flung open like the pressured valve of a steam cooker, and Sheriff fell like a cabbage. Mom sprinkled water hard on him. I stood there in fright, not knowing what was happening to him. Dad had arrived and after half an hour, he was revived. But his eyes were petrified and his lips had quivered in fright.

During dinner that day, Mum and Dad whispered about vacating the house. I remember protesting.

Since that day in the late 70s and ever after I chose to immortalize my walnut tree in 2020, cataclysmic changes have occurred in the Nilgiris, in my country, and in my life. Some for good, some for bad, some necessary, some inevitable, some unpalatable too.

But life moves on…

*"My dear Colonel, I have been in the Highlands for the last week. This is the finest country... It resembles I suppose Switzerland more than any other part of Europe... It freezes here every night, this morning we found ice in our Water chatties (*clay pots*)."*

– John Sullivan, 8th Jan 1819

(In his description of the Nilgiris)

The Nilgiri Puffs

Memory tied to a food experience can linger for a lifetime. One such memory, regarding a gastronomic déjà vu, surfaced when Dharmanna, our cook had served scrumptious vegetable puffs. It's a simple snack with an assortment of vegetables stuffed into a small crescent-shaped pouch of *maida* or wheat flour and fried. But of course, a distant cousin of the bakery puffs.

There are few delicacies, according to me, that equal a crispy, spicy, hot puff; for me, it's the best evening snack to munch on.

It's all the more special to have it in the Nilgiris with a cup of steaming tea, and with the winter chill playing on your nostrils and preening on your lips. Puffs have been a quick and delicious way I have discovered to appease my craving for something savoury. No wonder, I was nicknamed as the "puff boy." "Those puffs are little demons in your body," reprimanded my mom, when I showed no appetite for food. "Tempt him with puffs, he would even sell his birth right," glibly remarked one of my aunts. "A piece of puff would suffice when I threw tantrums," recounted my Dad.

Ganapathy Villas was a tiny roadside tea stall that used to sell puffs, vadas, and spicy pakoras in the evenings near our home. After a day's hectic work, usually, the local folks gathered here to smoke, chit-chat, relax and also have a bite of their choice.

In the evenings, while we sat together as a family in the living room, slowly and craftily like a lead singer, I used to initiate "Mummy… *pasikuthu… pasikuthu* (hungry.... hungry)," in a sing-song fashion. My brothers felt it convenient to join me in the chorus. "Prem is the culprit," inculpated my Mom. But the chorus grew vehement…

"Who knows what oil is used to fry those oil-soaked puffs?" blurted my Mom with a frown. She had dissuaded us from laying hands on such unhealthy stuff from the Ganapathy

Villas. But my Dad had always graciously yielded to his son's resolute and concerted 'sloganeering for snacks' and thus gladly parted with the bucks. Soon, I had stormed into Ganapathy Villas, leaving my Mom ranting on 'strict parenting' and 'healthy food habits'.

Gopal *ettan*, the owner of the tea shop, sat there grimly at the counter. A light brown shawl loosely hung around him. I have never seen him smile, but his nimble fingers had spun the newspaper cones, with astounding speed and deftness. I had curiously watched him spin and roll the puffs into the cones.

My granny had by then brewed the black jaggery coffee. How exultant we felt those days to leisurely linger as a family together. During summer, the windows were kept open with Dahlias and Chrysanthemums in different hues fluttering in our garden.

However, my indulgence in puffs did not cease. It had continued to stir my appetite. Today perhaps, psychologists in all certitude would have traced symptoms of eating disorder, or binge eating, or would have attributed it to 'emotional hunger'.

After a game of soccer or under the guise of having missed the school bus, I trotted the hillock to my Dad's office, near the popular 'Shinkows' from the Breeks fields, close to the Botanical Gardens.

My Dad's office in the head post office was on the first floor. The whole environment had changed in the wooden stairway that led there. It was like treading the British Raj. The wooden stairs were broad, dusty, and starved of polish.

The roof was ridden with cobwebs. It appeared that the stairs had never been spruced up after the British had left India. The hangover was thick with its musty odour, but strangely, I had seemed to be fond of it.

I had always ascended the stairs gently, with my little feet, pussy footing each step. I must have climbed it over a hundred times.

My Dad, I knew, would be busy with his accounts, and would never welcome any guest, even his son. I paused near the main door before passing through a grim, dismal passage. When I peeped like an elf, somebody noticing my presence would announce, "Rajan Sir, your junior is here." With a great sense of immediacy, my Dad would be present before me, pulling up his pants and adjusting his spectacles. He led me to the post office canteen, and like a lamb I would follow him.

The canteen could boast of only a few wooden tables, benches, and a cupboard displaying the vadas, puffs, and *bajjis* (fritters). Bereft of any utterances, puffs and tea would appear on my table. I guess, I must have easily gobbled hundreds of puffs there. This persisted even during my graduation days. My dad had never grown weary, offering me puffs.

I had moved away from the hills during the late 80s and my dad had retired in the late 90s.

Down through the years and the seasons, destiny made me feel the ebb and flow of Brahmaputra in Assam and plodded me into the territory of the Asiatic Lions in Gir National Park in Gujarat. Within fifteen days of my transfer to Gujarat, which was a huge blow by itself, to bear the brunt of another arrow cruelly unleashed on my chest was rather difficult. My dad had succumbed to a cardiac arrest, probably in anticipation of my transfer to the South, which had heavily weighed on his mind. I was a fond son to my dad.

In Shimoga, I have now lived for seven seasons, watching the peepul tree stripping itself in autumn and arraying again in splendour on its own in spring. I have gazed at the Siberian storks and the pin-legged flamingos dazzle the sky during winters.

Last summer, I visited the Nilgiris and I was there in the post office canteen after several decades with my friend, Moses. In the hills, things are immutable unless man indulges his commercial interests. It seemed that time had startlingly stood still in the canteen. The same tables and benches were arranged in the same order. The recent whitewash had lent the walls a brighter flash.

Swayed by sentiment, I was particular to sit in the same place, in the same position. The very same snacks, and of course my favourite puffs had stared at me from the wooden cupboards.

We ordered puffs and tea. Before that, I had excused myself with an irresistible urge to climb the wooden stairs.

Climbing the same wooden stairs with the same musty odour was like mounting the hill of a generation too long ago. No more pussy footing, but I never wanted to glide over it either. I was conscious of each step. Each step I had savoured, each step I had stared. One step at a time, I had stepped up laden with nostalgia but prodded with the piety of a pilgrim.

It was difficult to hasten forward with memories pregnant in your mind. However, I had reached the door. I knew I could advance no further.

I stood there near the door for a few seconds in solemn silence. I was like a hungry mendicant, wanting to knock on the door for alms, but with several constraints holding me back.

Moses had waited for me in the canteen. I joined him. A vivid picture of my dad, short, bespectacled, clad in a grey coat, buttoned with a protruding belly, stood there before me, with one hand splayed in his pocket and another holding the glass of tea, sipping, and enthused with his son over his favourite puffs...

To break the silence, Moses said, "Prem, Uncle had a glorious finish." I nodded my head and replied, "Yes," with my throat choked and my eyes moistened. For the first time, perhaps the puffs were distasteful.

Yesterday at dusk, I sat with both my sons over half a dozen of puffs on the dining table specially made for the occasion. While I had narrated the tale of the Nilgiri puffs, in the background we overheard the rapturous hoot of the peafowl bellowing a plaintive song. The red-whiskered bulbuls were piping a song of peace and happiness. The cacophonic flock of jungle babblers had hopped in our backyard with their perpetual furious looks, hunting for their food. My sons were listening with rapt attention, perhaps hooked more to my story of the Nilgiri puffs than to the puffs in their hands, devoid of their usual nonchalance.

The sun had glinted on the heap of puffs before it had slanted down on the Sahyadri hills that overlook our backyard in Gajanur.

"Sometimes nostalgia hits me so hard
And my memory is too vivid, too real
Sometimes I feel it all again
I hear it all again
Sometimes I find my cheeks wet with
Tears wetted by smiles of times
Lost forever to me."

– Willow Teagan

The Girl with The Pitcher

"*Prem Anna*, the memory of that evening in the pine forest still springs goosebumps all over my body," said Suchi in a hushed voice, in a surprise call yesterday; perhaps after three decades or more. Quite younger than me, Suchi was my neighbour and a childhood friend in the H.P.F Township, in the Nilgiris. She now lives in Michigan, in the US. Her soulful voice combined with her affable smile, and her flowery face added an endearment to it. We had a special bond between us and I had a sense of responsibility for her.

Although she is a mom of three kids now, she is still the same, small, cheerful child, balancing a pitcher on her waist, and making bustling trips effortlessly to fill her pitcher to the brim. Sometimes, we had gone out to fetch water from the guest house or the garage or our school.

With Suchi beside me, I neither felt the weight of the pitcher nor the distance. She had the aura and grace to enliven my days. We had many little things to share and exchange. She had chattered about her friends, her cousins, and the mischiefs of her brothers. She would confide her secrets, and I would spill mine to keep her in good humour, which was a boon to her. We would plan small adventures and exchange goodies.

I had awaited in the late evenings to go out with little Suchi, clad in her bright yellow skirt, strewn with flowery designs, and a pitcher in hand. For the thirty minutes we had conversed yesterday, we were transported to our childhood in the Nilgiris. There are few things in life as enthusing as meeting childhood friends. It's all the more special if it's in the hills. Life in the hills is close-knit and full of camaraderie, fun, and adventure. The mesmerizing bluish hue hovering over the hills has a mysterious power to bind the folks. Suchi and I were nature's kids and we had thrived in its bosom. We joyously conversed about our common friends, neighbours and our childhood adventures. "Anna, I had visited the Nilgiris last December, and I had taken my children to Pykara Lake, the botanical garden, and Doddabetta Peak, and my children enjoyed the horse ride," she said.

Suchi's home was the first of the four families in a lined house which was a mini–South India by itself. The sunlight had lit the creamy-yellow tint of the smitten wood that lay on the wall in a row beside her home. With her parents working in the company, Suchi was left under the care of her maternal aunt.

Krishna Ettan, her dad, was everyone's favourite. He generously shared the Kerala delicacies. During Onam, special Sadhya lunch was served on banana leaves. As Suchi grew, she visited me in the afternoons at my home during weekends and vacations. She filled the void of a younger sister in me. As a child, I had a certain claim over her. She was a buoyant butterfly flitting and spreading her hues before me. Her radiant smile, her sweet intense eyes, and her friendly overtures drew me towards her. She shared her favourite salt biscuits, coconut balls, and plain cakes, but it was her touch that gave them yet another distinctive flavour.

We had plucked pear near the rivulet, and had relished it seated on a rock, with the chill and gurgling rivulet romping with our feet, in oblivion to the raptures of time.

We had played in the summer shower and followed the gliding butterflies. Our ears were tuned to the Nilgiri martin and the robin in the Sholas. We prepared ice candies from the frost. Crushing the tender eucalyptus and cypress leaves, we inhaled the aroma from each other's fingers. We stole carrots and turnips from the fields.

An unforgettable adventure awaited us on one vacation. We had a walk to the pine forest near our home in the evening. The pine forest is always tranquil and picturesque with its soaring pines. We rolled on the natural mattress of the needle-shaped pine leaves. The slant of the fading sunlight had filtered through, bringing a glow to little Suchi's face. We gathered the cones in the pine forest. We gazed at the fly agaricus mushrooms with their bright red hue. There was an eerie silence but for the intermittent twitters of the laughing Nilgiri thrush. Suchi suggested we play hide and seek. "Close your eyes and count fifty," I said. Soon, I had crawled inside a thick bush. There was no way for little Suchi to find me out. After considerable time, the silence in the pine forest was scary; I gently wriggled out and looked for her. I shouted, "Hey Suchi," in all directions. But my voice only echoed to me. I ran down the sloping strip of the pine forest frantically, but Suchi remained elusive. The sunlight had turned thinner. I was growing jittery. Where did she go? Should I run back home and check for her or get help? Should I stay and wait in the forest? A hundred ideas, doubts, and fears throttled my mind. I yelled out in utter despair. The first spell of evening chill began. I could feel it in my nostrils. I was hungry, thirsty, and tired. I saw a rabbit in a little distance, hunted after by a fox. What if other wild animals begin to appear? I will become easy prey to leopards. Where is my Suchi? Is she caught in some swamp or did she drown in the nearby lake? Is she struck down by wild thorns? Is she eaten up by some wild animal? My heart was beating as the last streak of light was turning dimmer, and the pine forest and Sholas lay like a huge monster, left all to myself. My body sweated profusely and began to shiver. Once again little Suchi's face began haunting me. Oh! How much I craved for her at that moment. In a last-ditch effort, I mustered all my strength and whistled, but alas, my whistles went rippling and got lost in the forest.

When I had almost given up, in the dusk, with visibility becoming dimmer inside the forest, in the silence, sounded a human voice in a whimper. With all my senses tuned to the voice, I thought "Could it be Suchi's? Oh! I wished it could be hers." My feet instinctively hastened towards the voice, with no time at hand. The darkness didn't deter me. The thistles and thorns did not hamper me. Like a little soldier, I chased after the human voice, amidst the shrubs, the stunted trees, and yet she was not visible.

The sound was now distinct, "*Anna, Anna.*" Eventually, I traced her lying behind a rock in the bush, almost in a semi-conscious state. I gently touched her and her body was aching, and was sweating profusely. I wiped the sweat from her face and she could recognize me. Her lips were dry and she now began to weep. I held her tenderly. "Suchi, what happened? Where had you been?" She did not respond but her face began to beam. "*Anna... Anna...*" She was stammering. But her words were choked. I slowly lifted her hand and leaning on me, I led her slowly. She wouldn't let go of my hand. Her hands were chill. She was totally drained of her strength. Within fifteen minutes, we had reached our homes, just in time.

For the next week, Suchi fell sick. None knew, till this day, what exactly had happened. After one week, both of us sat in the maidan and she started, "Anna, I went to the far end of the pine forest that day seeking you. I looked everywhere and suddenly I was overcome by fear. Fortunately at that moment, when I thought I was alone, I saw a woman who later said she was Brinda crossing my path and going across the Sholas. I called out to her in desperation. She was a pleasant woman with a welcome smile. 'Hello, dear child, what are you up to at this time of the day?' In a cordial manner, she initiated a conversation. 'Aunty, I am trying to find out my Anna. We have been playing hide and seek.' 'But it isn't safe for you to be alone', she sounded so caring. 'In fact, a little while ago I noticed a boy in the distance with his brown T-shirt and black half-trousers trotting towards the lake. That must be your Anna, I guess. He must have gone to the shooting set, where Kamala Hassan and Sridevi are being shot for a scene in the upcoming Tamil film. I am on my way to watch the Stars, come, I shall take you. He must be there.'

I followed after her in implicit obedience. We passed through the thorny thickets and twisted trunks, with many branches. I saw the ferns climbing onto the trees. We passed through the myrtle, shrubs, mosses, and a small crackling stream. There was a diverse species of grass, and dwarf trees in the Sholas. 'Look child, Sholas are the giant sponges of Nature. They feed lakhs of perennial springs and keep them teeming during the severest of the summers downhill. Almost all the major rivers of South India originate in the Sholas'. Brinda Aunty was quite informative. 'I worked in the company those days'. She quickly pointed to a rare bird and said, 'That's a wood cock, a rare migratory bird. Listen to its beep, child. It comes all the way from the Himalayas during winter.' She said she was a naturalist. She told me that she knew both of our mums. Now within a few minutes, we were in the shooting set. There was quite a crowd, jostling to watch the film stars. I was excited. Brinda Aunty was restlessly moving here and there, in a bid to have a closer view of the actors. While Kamala Hassan was friendly, Sridevi seemed to be withdrawn. My eyes never darted from Sridevi. She was a stunning beauty.

'They are the best pair ever', Brinda Aunty remarked.

Soon the shooting was done, both the actors moved away in a car and the crowd melted away in no time.

'Where is your *Anna*?' Brinda Aunty smiled at me. 'I couldn't find him here, Aunty'. With no one left, Aunty suggested, 'Child, the lake is not too far, let's check whether we can find him there'. Within another ten minutes, we crisscrossed the Sholas, the rhododendrons and the bishop wood trees stood in mute silence. We took a small path that led us to the lake. After crossing the rolling grass, the lake was visible. The water was bluish and crystal clear. I was wary of going near the lake. 'Aunty, my parents have always instructed me to not go near the lake. I have heard that this lake had swallowed several folks. I am afraid Aunty.' 'Come on child', Brinda Aunty convinced me. 'I am there with you. Follow me.' The moment she noticed the lake, I saw her gliding towards it. I found it difficult to keep pace with her. When we reached the lake, I stood there and didn't want to move further. Beyond the lake, another strip of Shola forest and then the hills arose in the distance. The sun was about to set. Brinda Aunty gesticulated. 'Come, let's feel the water and have a small dip'.

While I didn't budge, she was wading through the water, to my surprise. She suddenly turned towards me and I thought I saw something strange about her eyes and face. In a twinkling of an eye, like an alligator, she plunged into the water and never returned. I yelled out, 'Brinda Aunty! Brinda Aunty!' I stood there dumbstruck, I became numb, and my body began to tremble. I hardly remember what happened in the next few minutes that followed." When Suchi narrated the incident, her body began to tremble. We decided to keep the incident a secret. To this day nobody knows about it.

That night, I couldn't get a wink of sleep. The pine forest, the lake, and Brinda Aunty kept haunting my mind. After a day or two, I asked my mum, "Mummy, do you remember anyone named Brinda who had worked with you long ago?" She paused, what seemed like an uneasy pause. "Poor Brinda, she tragically died in a drowning incident in the lake several years ago."

Yesterday Suchi confided, "Even after three decades and more whenever I have stood before any lake anywhere, be it the lake Michigan, or the Tahoe, the spectre of Aunt Brinda draped in her pink saree, cream sweater and a black vanity bag with a pink rose neatly pinned on her hair with her parting grin flashes before me."

"The songs she wobbled, burbled like a brook
Over rocks and hills, the clouds in her hook;
Her brown glasses slid over her nose tip,
How cute her eyes rolling upon her cherry lip."

– R Premkumar

Sunshine on the Mountains

Far away in the salubrious Nilgiri Hills, the evening was moist and chill. The bell rang and the students tumbled out from the corridors of the school. It seemed that they were elated, that yet another day was over. Learning, it appeared was not a joyous experience to most of them. The red and grey company buses, designated for school trips, were ready with their humming engines.

Interestingly, the playfield was already abuzz with the bounces of the football and the dribbles of the basketball, with the intermittent whistles of Mr. Kumariah, the P.T. Master, whom the children had feared and adored. He had encouraged them to play merrily to their hearts' content. It was in the playfield that the children redeemed their losses on the academic front. There were no boundaries and limits set forth in the field. Children sported without inhibitions, whatsoever.

Near the dispensary, a boy awaited in all eagerness with an Enid Blyton in his hand. He was hanging out long after his schoolmates had left for their homes. Surprisingly, he had abandoned his favourite football play that day. The ill-kept tiny garden at the entrance of the dispensary flaunted a handful of white and red dahlias and yellow chrysanthemums, despite the stifling weeds and bushes.

The little boy was absorbed in the ivy creeper that had trailed on the front walls of the dispensary. It was a splendid sight to see the handiwork of nature. His curious eyes were also more than serious, obviously searching and waiting for something.

A teacher who passed by questioned the boy, "Hey, what are you watching and waiting for?" He was reprimanded to get away to his home and prepare for the forthcoming Unit Test. How would he explain himself to the teacher, the boy wondered. A little above, on the highway, a wearied red Mysore bus rumbled and halted. A turbaned passenger alighted with a heap of overpowering coconuts.

The coveted, glossy, light brown Ambassador flashed past, with the ever-immaculate C.M.D. of HPF, Mr. P.R.S. Rao to the guest house. The proud employees were pouring out in a deluge, after their shifts. Those were the heydays of the Indu Film factory.

The boy was still rooted to the same place. After what seemed a long wait, Lilly, the little girl emerged from the dispensary muffled with a multi-coloured scarf and a school bag. Her eyes were watery and her lips were dry, and paleness hung on her otherwise cheerful and bubbly countenance.

Her voice sounded gruff, with a bout of fever and cold. "Hi," she greeted the little fellow, with a half-smile. Her greetings splashed a rainbow on his mind. Overwhelmed, he tottered as he drew nigh to her and enquired about her health. He gently slipped the Enid Blyton into her hands. Soon, the ambulance arrived and she quickly darted into it, bidding a sudden and silent 'bye' to him.

Oh! How he wished that she would have lingered longer. His eyes were glued to the little princess and followed her long after the ambulance chugged and faded away.

Little Lilly saddled with a school bag trod to school every day through the muddy, winding paths. Her home stood behind the lake and beside the Shola forest. Eagerly on her way to school each day, her plaits swung as she braved the wintry chill, the boisterous winds, and the torrential monsoon rain. The summer breeze gently played on her cheeks and eyes. There was an inexplicable loveliness about the impressive way she spoke, smiled, and carried herself. Excelling both in studies and sports, an all-rounder, she was a budding orator and a favourite singer of her school. Trim on her school uniform, interestingly her brown glasses slid over her nose tip and her protruding eyes seemed as if they rolled over her lips. She was gregarious, amiable, and a passionate reader. The little boy took upon himself the self-imposed but sweet responsibility of lending books to her from the school library, pandering to her taste. He proffered her with all the treasures of books like a mother eagle, and like the eaglets, she devoured it fondly. This he did to win her affection and please her as he was under a spell of tender fondness, a weighing claim and a certain devotion to her.

The school lay like a monster in paralysis. A few crows and mynahs were on their return flight to their nests. The blanket of dust that had enshrouded the empty field raised by the busy feet of children began settling down. The golden glow in the sky was a master stroke by the sun before it parted.

The little boy reluctantly dragged himself to his home and remained sulky throughout, hardly coming to terms with his surge of emotions. But thoughtfully, he whispered an innocent but sincere prayer for his little friend, before he retired to his bed.

In his dreams, Lily floated with radiance, with her frilled pink frock. That was the year for the rare flowers of Neelakurinji, which bloomed once in twelve years in the Shola forest and hills of the Western Ghats in the Nilgiris. They mounted the verdant hills, hand in hand with limitless bliss and were lost to the resplendent glory of the purplish-blue blossoms.

The following day little Lily had hopped to school with her marble eyes and sang "*Una Paloma Blanca*" by George

Baker, "When the Sun shines on the mountains," and swept him away to the skies and beyond…

That was four decades ago.

Life is a beautiful album of transience and we are bound by what it leaves behind.

Like every girl, the little lily was lost in the inevitable ritual of womanhood, marriage, motherhood, and family. He never got to see her sprightly self ever again, but his soul is still aflame with her song that transports him to the Nilgiri Hills cloaked with *Neelakurinji* blossoms, like the sunshine on the mountains.

"Be not inhospitable to strangers lest they be angels in disguise."

– George Whitman

Uncle Captain

It must have been around 6 am in that winter morn, in the Nilgiris. The frost had carpeted the grass with its white hues. The lake in the distance was placid and still. Sparrows, mynahs and crows flittered and chattered restlessly. Muffled with a monkey cap and tracksuit, I was engaged in the usual practice sessions, all set to become an accomplished athlete.

My favourite playfield during the early morn and late evening wore a deserted look but was bustling with sports activities during the daytime. I had always played to my heart's content and was a champion in sports. After a game of football, I tried my stint in basketball. Mr. Kumariah, My P.T. Master, strategically made us play with the girls' basketball team; no wonder they were a formidable team. After basketball, I also had my share of playing volleyball. Oh! I had detested studies, but was very fond of sports and play. I had played to redeem my losses in academics. My Maths teacher, Mr. Ramachandran's remark that I was a below-average student still rattles in my mind to this day.

That morning in the mist, I saw a diminutive figure alighting the steps to the pathway alongside the field leading to the officers' residence, which stood above and beyond the playfield. He clapped his hands, pointed his fingers, and called out to me. I promptly responded, and in a few seconds, I presented myself before him. He was clad in a white and blue tracksuit and a brown velvet hat; he was stout but fit. He was handsome with his silvery grey beard and curiously piercing eyes, but it only brought a sense of discomfort for a fifteen-year-old. He greeted me Good morning, which I reciprocated with a quiver in my voice.

"What is your name?" There was a sternness in his interrogation.

"Uncle, I am Prem."

"Are you an athlete?"

I responded, "Yeah."

"Do you practice every day?"

I replied, "Yeah."

"Rubbish, what is this yeah," he angrily reprimanded, seemingly irritated with my spurt of yeahs.

"Where are you studying and in which class?"

I replied, "I am a student of KV in IXth standard."

"What is this basket over your head?" he questioned, pointing to my hair. "You look like a real junglee. Who is your principal?"

"She is Mrs Indira Prithviraj." By now, I was trembling.

"I will make a complaint to your principal for growing a junglee in her school."

My tongue was dried up.

"I am Captain Vasudevan." He sounded proud and there was an air of superiority and confidence. "Come, Prem. Could you help me find Mr. Narayan Singh's home? I believe it was somewhere here."

"Yes, Uncle. Naval and Adarsh, his sons are my friends. We play together." Mr. Singh's home was the second home in a row of four independent houses. There were a few cypress and eucalyptus trees which we had to cross before we could reach the entrance of the gate. When we went inside, Uncle Captain was perturbed by the forlorn look inside the compound. The weeds had overgrown. There was a big bush in the space for the garden. The rose plant had no roses; evidently, it was not tended to. A few drooping dahlias were peeping out, nothing more. I was instructed to knock on the door, while he chose to stay away. I knocked on the door, and stood there, waiting for the door to be opened. He furiously chided, "Get back! What a mannerless boy are you! Don't you know that you have to maintain a distance after you knock on someone's door?"

I said, "Sorry Uncle," and repeated it at least three times, as there was no response.

Uncle Captain quipped, "It looks like nobody is there." He asked me to confirm with the neighbour, who was Girish, another friend of mine whose mom was a medical officer in the health centre.

"Uncle, Mr. Singh and family are out of station. They had left for Rajasthan on an emergency visit. It will be another week or more before they arrive." Uncle Captain surprisingly did not show any semblance of disappointment but gave an ambiguous smile that was hard to decipher.

As we returned, Uncle Captain questioned me regarding my studies. I couldn't give a proper answer. Uncle asked me a few algebra questions. I never knew the answer.

"How is your GK?"

I remained silent.

"Who is the present Army Chief?"

Again in embarrassment, I had put my head down.

"It's General Kotikalapudi Venkatakrishnarao." He insisted that I should repeat it thrice. Deep down in my heart,

I was wishing hard that I should get away from this ordeal and escape for life. But the next question was shot at me.

"Have you read Wordsworth's famous poem 'Daffodils?'"

I nodded my head.

"Prem, nothing seems to be there in your head." He cautioned me that he would be meeting up with my principal in a day or two. He quickly trotted back on the same road. Oh! That moment brought a whiff of relief, but never in my life I had been so much exposed. I was stripped of my little ego. I was scared. I was furious, embarrassed, and hurt.

The same evening, I rushed to the salon and the jungle over my head was cleared. The hairdresser was astonished indeed. My heart was throbbing as the slices of hair went crashing down. I had cherished them all the while. I had spent hours before the mirror setting my hair. During the night, I tied a rubber band over my basket of hair and anticipated a miracle in the morning. However, the basket over my head did never budge. I read the 'Daffodils' and committed to my memory. My dad rejoiced that eventually, his son had turned over a new leaf. But my friends were unhappy. It meant defeat not only for me but for them too. At that age, we felt good breaking rules. All the while, I did not utter a word about Uncle Captain to anyone for some unknown reason.

The next day in the morning assembly, my principal Mrs Indira Prithviraj, addressed the students and instructed that they should be well-behaved and earn a good reputation in the community. My principal was a middle-aged, tall, and well-built lady. She was a strict disciplinarian and warned that severe action would be initiated against children who violate the rules of the school and bring disrepute to the institution. I felt that the whole school was watching me. There was a clogging burden of guilt weighing me down. I was sure that Uncle Captain had already met with the principal. I was disturbed the whole day and was anxious about being summoned to the principal's chamber at any time. That afternoon there was a staff meeting, after which I sensed that all my teachers were staring at me. I could not carry myself to the field. I was there in my home by 4 pm.

The following day, I had an uneasy feeling. I had feigned sickness and avoided going to school. Gran looked after me well. She toasted bread for breakfast. In the afternoon, I was advised to restrict myself to rasam and rice. But I stole bitter gourd curry and gobbled it. Granma's dishes were irresistible. I was imagining what would have happened at school. In the evening, Ramesh and Murali, my friends called on me to enquire about my absence from school. They said that our English teacher was enquiring about me. Murali chided me, "*Parama* (that's what he used to call me), what happened, why did you choose to have a close haircut?" I did not have a reply. He remarked, "You are like a sheep that is shorn of its hair." He meant to say that I was ugly.

The basket of hair, which I had cherished had gone, and with that, a portion of my childhood and its fancies were chopped off. The basket of hair was my way of establishing my identity. It was a symbol of my youth and an ache for recognition.

The news was abuzz in the school that Adarsh and Naval's house was burgled. But didn't I visit Mr. Narayan Singh's home with Uncle Captain? All was well, I thought to myself and kept the whole incident to myself.

Not many days after this incident, The *Hindu* newspaper carried a report "Burglars nabbed in HPF Township," with a picture inserted with it. It was a close shot of the three handcuffed burglars. It had barely taken me a split second to unmistakably recognize the kingpin, whose face I was so obsessed with for a couple of days. Uncle Captain stood with his accomplices with the same air of confidence. The child in me felt a sense of rude shock, relief, liberation, and of course a tinge of sympathy.

To this day, I have a close haircut, I can quote 'Daffodils', and have read the works of Wordsworth, and own a copy of the *Golden Treasury* and keep visiting it. I also maintain a decent distance whenever I knock at someone's door. Ironically, I owe it all to Uncle Captain.

"The time I spent in the jungles held unalloyed happiness for me, and that happiness I would now gladly share. My happiness, I believe, resulted from the fact that all wildlife is happy in its natural surroundings. In nature there is no sorrow, and no repining."

– Jim Corbett

Lost in the Jungle

The trip to Moyar, a tiny hamlet in Nilgiris, is one of those special memories of childhood that you reminisce about all your life. We had just finished our tenth-grade exams and wanted to chill. Four of us planned this adventure. We were hardly sixteen and every ounce of our being ached for a change from the tedium.

Vijayanand whom we called Viji mooted the idea of visiting Moyar. We readily agreed, but our immediate challenge was to persuade our parents to give consent.

"A car had recently plunged into Moyar River and three were dead," stated Ramesh's Dad with concern. He was a newspaper worm, who had all the news at his fingertips.

My mother pointed out, "Moyar is not a safe place, the jungles abound with wildlife and there have been numerous incidents of human–elephant conflicts. It is life-threatening to venture into the jungles." My grandfather, who was a hunter himself, recounted his sighting of the big cat, stretching in the sunlight, on an afternoon.

Murali's father added, "The Moyar River flows into the gorge below Theppakadu in a boisterous and roaring waterfall. These are unsafe places for children." Our parents dissuaded us from going on the trip.

However, we devised plans and strategies and eventually got the nod from them. Oh! How delighted and enthralled we were at the prospect of this adventure! We looked forward with great expectations.

Viji assured us that he would arrange the forest guest house in Moyar, where his relatives were the caretakers.

The joy of adventuring with friends, the excitement of exploring a new place, and the freedom to be on our own ushered in a sense of emancipated feeling that a teenager cherishes.

Ramesh had big soulful eyes and wavy hair, mature for his age; he was an atheist with communist leanings. He was studious and emerged as one of the toppers of the class. Both of us shared our passion for poetry and athletics and had endless debates about the existence of God. Murali was a cricketer and rode his black BSA cycle with a style that was unique to him. He grew ruddy when he lost his temper with our class girls. Murali was handsome, fair with curly hair. He conversed in Badaga at home while Ramesh spoke Malayalam. My mother tongue was Tamil. Our homes were open for friends.

Being under the spell of wanderlust, we adventured, cycled, sported, visited the public library, gallivanted all over the HPF Township, strolled across the lake and lost ourselves in the golf links and pine forest in the Nilgiris. We frequented our favourite spots, being nature's fond children. We did have our childhood infatuations. The evenings we spent gladly with our teacher at her home, she called us Tirumurthies.

The momentous occasion arrived and we had set out, all the four of us to Moyar. We took the minibus which drove through Thalaikundah and Kalahatti. The roads were winding and narrow. Since we were hill children, it did not bother us, in fact, we enjoyed meandering through the hills and valleys.

The Kalahatti Ghat road is a narrow and single road that winds itself down to Masinagudi. It is a steep shortcut road to Mysore that connects to Theppakadu through the 36-hairpin-bend drive.

The road was hazardous, but it was still a real treat for budding hodophiles, with foliage on either side. The deciduous trees in the moist teak forest and bamboo shoots offered a lifetime experience with its fresh air as we descended into Masinagudi. Masinagudi provides an abundance of nature's finest views of the river, streams, rich forests, and rich flora and fauna.

Viji was our guide; for the next three days, we would be at his disposal. The bus halted at Masinagudi for tea. The drive from Masinagudi to Moyar was a short but scenic drive, with the river branch flowing alongside the road. A tusker came close to our bus but our driver with his experience managed to steer away to safety. We spotted a herd of deer and a peacock. The forest, with its luxurious growth of flowering and non-flowering trees, had a special charm. The Moyar River had turned muddy but had gently meandered through the steep canyon resembling a giant serpent. Soon we reached Moyar; it is a small village around 11 km from Masinagudi. This is the last village on this route. The whole road length of 11 km between Masinagudi and Moyar does not have any inhabitation. Hence, it is exciting to drive through this road. We spotted deer, elephants, and Indian gaur. The village of Moyar is scenic, where a lake forms its heart.

Viji lead us into their relative's home which was situated amidst the forest. It was his maternal uncle, his wife, and their daughter who welcomed us. His uncle was middle-aged, clad in a dhoti; his wife seemed friendly and a flibbertigibbet. Their daughter, a little older than us, was draped in a pink half-saree, which was altogether glorious. Her gestures, smiles, and looks, put a jinx on us. She was like a little fairy dazzling in the jungle. It appeared that the family was delighted to host us. They conversed in Kannada but spoke to us in Tamil. We were offered a cup of tea and soon lunch was ready. The lunch was vegetarian but sumptuous. It started with holige, smeared with ghee. All three of us were shy boys and spoke less but enjoyed the food.

We were waiting to get into the forest guest house that Viji had promised us, but to our bad luck, few official guests had arrived and we couldn't be accommodated. However, we were relegated to the outhouse which was meant for drivers and servants. We happily accepted it; Murali was cracking jokes about it. Viji was disappointed that he couldn't keep his word. The evening was spent loitering and exploring the new place around the forest guest house.

This region seemed a significant pocket of biodiversity and an important migration corridor for elephants, Indian gaurs and ungulates like spotted deer, black bull and sambhar. Starting from Gudalur to Sathyamangalam, it's a tapestry of hills interspersed with deep gorges and the valley is a chosen landscape for a plethora of flora and fauna.

We could listen to innumerable birds making distinct calls. As the night began to fall, the birds, of various sizes and colours, flew past us. We hardly knew their names then. Mynahs, crows, sparrows, and parrots were in plenty. We also noticed many eagles. Later on, I learnt that the Nilgiris represents a unique landscape within the Western Ghats owing to its topographical climate and habitat features and this particular region is an important wintering area for several migrant raptors.

We had a quick dinner and we left for the outhouse. We had to sleep on the floor but we enjoyed it. We chatted till midnight; we discussed our classmates and our teachers. We were strictly instructed not to leave our room as wild boars, elephants, and Indian gaurs came close. How we wished we sighted them in the night; we kept the windows open and were eager, almost awaiting the sudden appearance of wildlife. It was a full moon, and all night I could hear the soothing sound of a brook trickling past. There was also unending background music scored by the crickets. We had anticipated the sound of some wild animals, maybe the roar of a tiger, but the continuous soundtrack provided by the insects deafened our ears. We cracked our usual jokes, we pulled the legs of each other, and we gossiped about our classmates and friends and had a great time. Interestingly, late at midnight, we heard a volley of grunts, evidently from a herd of wild boars close to our room.

Murali instantly reacted and screamed "*Hey Panni, bajji da,*" in a slip of his tongue. We had nicknamed Viji, as *bajji*. *Panni* means pig in Tamil. We could not but burst out in laughter. This is a classic joke, which has stayed with us all along.

The following day, Viji lead us into the jungle. We had to cross a rivulet that led into the Moyar River. The Moyar River is one of the tributaries of Bhavani. It originates from Moyar and forms a natural line separating the state of Karnataka and Tamil Nadu. It also separates the forests of Bandipur National Park and Mudumalai Sanctuary.

The monkeys were making faces and the langurs were apprehensive to see four teenagers sneaking into their territory. The chattering increased, but we were determined to proceed further. We laid hands on wild fruits. The sun was ablaze, and the forest was dry. In the distance, we noticed an elephant twisting its trunk.

We went as far as we could go into the jungle, the four of us. Every bush and every small cave alerted us. We suspected the hideout of either the crafty leopard, a bear or a tiger. We were apprehensive about whether we would be caught unawares. Leopards especially are ambush hunters. We were conscious of the dangers in the jungle; we saw scorpions, brown recluse spiders, snakes, vipers, and cobras; we spotted grey-headed bulbuls, a pair of woodpeckers knocking on the trees, hornbills flying past us, the Nilgiri woodpecker, and of course the song of the cuckoo.

The sambhar deer, the spotted deer came into our vicinity. We heard their alert calls. Ramesh recalled Anderson's books on his encounters with a man-eater and rogue elephants. The stories "the black rogue of Moyar Valley," and "the call of the man-eaters" were profoundly absorbing and sometimes scaring too. The black rogue was a bull elephant that trampled people to death in the Moyar Valley. Anderson recounts how he and his American friend, a photographer, ran into this rogue elephant and came precariously within inches of its deadly trunk.

We encountered a herd of elephants, led by the matriarch and several herds of Indian gaurs. Oh! It was awesome, to watch wildlife in their natural habitat.

The hills were refreshingly salubrious after a sharp shower. Our trail took us above the hills and along the valleys. We sighted fresh droppings, evidently of large mammals, but were clueless about the exact animal. We were exceedingly nervous. We never intended to spend a lot of time in the jungle. Viji's uncle warned us that we should restrain from venturing deep into the jungle, but even without our knowledge, we were way ahead. Something was alluring about the jungle. As we tread our way into the dense vegetation, the sweltering rays of the afternoon sun ignited the tree tops into a burst of greenery. We were hungry and thirsty. The gurgling streams of water quenched our thirst. We searched for wild fruits but found none. We played in the water, but none of us knew swimming. That was the disadvantage of hill children. We decided to return. As already it was half past three, we followed the trail that we came, and in a pool of water, to our utter amazement, we hit upon a herd of elephants bathing. We observed from a vantage spot, the pachyderms were enjoying their quality bathing time. They were cooling off, frolicking, wallowing, and splashing in the water. That was a fantastic and lifetime experience. We hurried our way back as the evening began to fall. We observed vultures, Brahminy kites, and black kites. We also sighted many strange birds but never knew to identify them. Oh! How I wished that a birder should have been there to educate us.

We noticed the carcass of a deer hidden inside a bush, but fortunately, it was not a fresh kill. Vultures were feasting on it. Murali suddenly said, "Wait… Wait…" He surveyed in all directions and alerted us, "Hey guys, we are traversing in the wrong path." We were anxious about getting back on time before darkness descends. We retraced our steps and then a trail of fresh pug marks began showing up and we examined them. It was startling; Viji said it was a Tiger and Ramesh said it could be a Leopard, but we were children, totally unarmed. What if we had to confront a predator? We decided to walk together and show our strength. The pug marks were still there, it was surely a solitary animal. We were shuddering and the palpitation increased. We lost the sense of direction. What if this trail was leading to the rows of hills that were up there? My heart was pounding. Will we ever reach our home safely? Will we get lost in this jungle? Amidst the anxiety, we realized this is one of the richest ecological areas, the luxurious forest that housed countless mammals, reptiles, and amphibians. They live unperturbed in these pristine forests. As we advanced, the paths meandered their way down to the valleys below. We walked and walked for what seemed like hours, without any rest and absolutely no breakthrough. Now the sun also began to sink, and with that, our hearts also sank. We began running, and as we ran, we felt that some wild animal was stalking us from behind. We were petrified, and we stopped. We never talked, but anxiety, fear, and fatigue were writ on each of our faces. Our little feet were aching. Survival and safety were our priority.

We saw various trees such as shrubs and swamps, moist deciduous sal, teak, and huge bamboo shrubs. It was just then a jungle cat listening to our footsteps plunged into the shrubs. We forgot about the pug marks until we noticed a huge bear rolling its way, in the distance. There was hardly any time with us. "Are we anywhere near or have we strayed," Murali questioned.

In the quiet of the dusk and the stillness of the jungle, in the distance, we heard the crackling of a stream. We decided we would move towards it. We took off.

The light grew dimmer. It appeared a swarm of night insects were storming behind us, deafening our ears. We ran for miles; it was already dark.

The faster we ran for our lives the farther the village seemed to distance itself. Murali was leading us, followed by Ramesh and myself. Viji tried catching us from behind as we sped on our heels negotiating the bushes, thistles, and rocks. The howls of the jackals struck an ominous note. The cricket began chirping vociferously and we stopped for a while. A pack of wild dogs suddenly emerged and were on their hunt. They paused, gave a curious glance at us but went about on their prowl. Darkness had set in and we felt dismal and exhausted. We continued onward negotiating the thorny bushes and the huge cactus; and lo and behold, we noticed the flicker of lights from the village. We surmised that it did not seem to be too far. We followed the banks of the rivulet, but there was no way we could cross.

The sound of the rivulet ushered in hope. For some time, we thought we would languish and perish. The rivulet drew us to itself. Our little feet were heading towards it. "Are we there yet," I yelled out, "I wish we were," replied Ramesh, but in reality, we were far away. "Damn it," blurted Murali in sheer frustration. Every inch of my body was aching. The croaks of an army of frogs suddenly blinded our eyes and stupefied us in fear. We were running ahead in the pitch dark. Now Ramesh was leading us with long strides followed by Murali, and behind me was Viji. The dim light of the village was brighter but still, we could not find a way out. As we advanced, we found two men carrying a huge log of wood, together. They never expected us during that time in the dark. We knew instinctively that they were up to some mischief. Later on, we realized, that they were smuggling teak out of the forest. "How do we enter the village?" We quietly quizzed them, and they guided us forward and showed us the way. Their presence enhanced our confidence and quelled our anxiety.

The villagers had erected a small creaky wooden structure to cross the rivulet. Eventually, we sighed a heave of relief. But it was short-lived. To our utter shock and dismay, we realized that Viji was missing. We assumed that he was behind us and keeping pace with us but where exactly we lost track of him was difficult to know. Little did we expect a mishap of this kind to strike. What to do? We were flummoxed by our friend gone missing. What would have happened to him? We were worried and anxiety played havoc. We stopped the two men and requested their help to save our lost friend. We pleaded with them. They asked us to shout out his name. Together all three of us, at the top of our voices yelled, "*Bajji Bajji Bajji.*" Our shouts reverberated in the jungle.

The bats were flying and foraging for their food. The hoots of the owl only frightened us further. We also heard piercing screams, shrieks, and wavering cries emerging from the jungle. With that mental state, these were only ominous signs.

The two men rebuked us harshly in filthy words in Tamil.

How dare you venture inside this dense jungle without a guide?

"Fools don't you have sense." Have you gone crazy? "*Muttal, Muttal, Pasangala*" (foolish, fellows).

Where do you think we can find him in these huge dark woods?

These words dispelled all hopes and brought despair. We knew that the jungle unleashed dangerous predators in the night. What must have happened to our dear Viji? "God please spare his life." The two men hid the log of wood in the bushes and directed us to follow them. We took the same trail where we left and retreated into the jungle. We could hardly see their faces. We heard a cacophonic concert of insects buzzing, frogs yelping, birds shrieking, and bats clicking. These spooky nocturnal sounds were spine-tingling.

With the little light from the torch they had, we plunged into the dark world yet again. It was apparent that these men were familiar with the terrains. We followed them for about thirty minutes. We heard close high-pitched barks, perhaps the wild dogs prowling in packs. We smelt some nauseating, pungent odour that could have been the territorial marks of one of the predators. The howls of the foxes were closing in. In the next few metres, we saw a pack of them trotting around. They were not put off by our presence.

Everything in the jungle was showing up but there were no signs of our beloved friend anywhere. After a long search in the bushes and rocks, the men were now giving up. They said we have to inform the police and forest department about the missing boy.

How would we face Viji's uncle and family? What shall we tell our parents? Would we ever go back to our homes?

Viji's handsome face was haunting me. He was fair, stout, and had wavy hair. There were already prominent traces of hair on his upper lip and his chin. His eyebrows were thick and he had big attractive eyes. Each time he met me, he praised me in a sing-song way, "Nationals… Nationals…" It appeared that he was proud of my achievements in athletics more than me. The two men continued yelling at us. "Forget your friend and report to the police immediately."

"Uncles, please save our friend," we pleaded. We could never digest returning without Viji with us. He was the brainchild of these adventures.

"Let us move on, it's getting late," said one of the men. When we had reluctantly turned, for a few seconds, there was total silence. It seemed that the jungle came to a standstill just for us. Ramesh said "Ssshhh… Wait… Wait… Wait… I can hear some human whimpers." He tuned his ears to the feeble voice. Confirming it, he straight away strode towards it and found alas! Viji lay fallen, on a thorny bush.

A glow worm had lit the dark. We called out "Viji! Viji!" We shook his body but there were only those whimpers. We lifted Viji from the bush and laid him down. One of the men quickly gave CPR. Continuous resuscitation helped Viji to revive. He gradually opened his eyes. He was semi-conscious. He was groaning, his body was chill. We found some bruises on his body. After a few minutes, we helped him to his feet, supported him on our shoulders and slowly walked until we reached the shaky bridge. We thanked the two men profusely for saving our friend and wanted to tip them but they outrightly rejected this offer and reprimanded us sarcastically, "Oh! You guys have grown so big that you want to tip us? Off you go, little thieves!" and slipped away into the dark.

After three decades, when we had met in Delhi at Ramesh's home, we had fond reminiscences of that experience in the Moyar jungle with goosebumps on our bodies. Ramesh trained himself to be a Naval Officer, Murali a top business executive and I chose to be an educationist.

After an exhaustive day and a night's rest, the next day we went to see the winch machine nearby. River Moyar is also the source of the Moyar powerhouse, which is a hydroelectric power station located at the bottom of the Moyar Gorge. We reached by a winch system from the plateau above. The experience in the winch was adventurous, exciting, and scary too. But that we were together made it interesting. Here we were hanging and sliding down on the rocks as the spools of cable were suspended down from above with the scorching summer sun blinding our eyes. The panoramic view, of the rows of hills on the other side, offered a really unforgettable lifetime experience.

On the final day, we visited Theppakadu Elephant Camp. It's the oldest elephant camp in Asia. Watching the pachyderms was a rewarding experience. The camp hosted several elephants that were trained under the guidance of forest authorities. We watched the elephants being fed, wallowing in rivers, and obeying the commands of the mahout. The elephants were fed on a mix of horse gram ragi, and jaggery, which were well cooked and made into a 10 kg ball. The mahouts lifted the balls to the mouth of the elephants, who had kept it wide open like a gate. The pachyderms devoured two or three of these balls at a time and tossed their trunks in delight.

"Running the extra mile, exercising enormous patience, reaching out to the last child, and bringing a ray of hope are the marks of an inspiring teacher."

– R Premkumar

When I Found Her

My childhood idol, my first love, was my English teacher in high school. She was barely twenty-five and I was sixteen. She was fair, frolicsome, nimble, slim, and stunningly gorgeous. I admired her like no one else. I had love, reverence, and adoration for her. When my classmates and friends grumbled things against her, I took fierce protests. The bond that I have with her through the decades cannot be defined in words but has stood the test of time.

Our school in Indunagar in the Nilgiris was bound by the Sholas and Pine forests, and a stream below crackled to the lake that lay in close proximity. We saw fish and tadpoles swim. The scent of eucalyptus permeated the air. The parents of our school were employees of Hindustan Photo Films, and all, including our teachers, lived in the sprawling HPF Township. Since it is a Central school, we had teachers drawn from the entire country, and periodic transfers were inevitable, but we developed a pan-India perspective.

It was in my IX grade that my teacher got to teach me. Her classes were interesting and each day I looked forward to it with certain anticipation. While her charm struck my sight her merit appealed to my soul. She had something magical about her personality to keep her students spellbound in class. Her expertise in the subject and teaching style, combined with her natural sense of humour, made her a teacher with a touch of class. She articulated in English with an easy elegance that was amazing.

I was not a promising student, but she bestowed enormous affection and confidence in me. While my Maths teacher, once angrily rebuked me as a below-average boy, my English teacher never gave up on me but invested her time and energy in a slow learner. How thrilled I felt as a teenager to receive a greeting card on my birthday, asking me to guess the sender. Of course, I did guess, but it was the best ever gift I could ever receive. I was overwhelmed at that tender age.

Draped in a sari, she appeared graceful and elegant. The light brown open sweater, with two pockets, with her hands splayed out into them, and stalking up and down in the class with her own characteristic style, was a visual treat. I could not take my eyes off her. I devoured every word that was uttered in the class, with implicit obedience and as gospel truth.

While she read every word of what we wrote in our tests and exams, she would never be satisfied with our performance. We were confident about English, but she was all the while raising the bar, in a bid to upgrade us to the next level. The tests were testing times indeed, as she was put off by our performance. She had a good teaching practice of reading the best answers to the class, and how proud I felt when my essay on penguins featured.

She was an avid reader, with a book in her hand always, and it was inspiring at that age to be introduced to great classics of Shakespeare, Dickens, Hardy, Emily Bronte, A.J. Cronin, P.G Wodehouse and others.

She taught us Tagore's short story 'Castaway,' which left an indelible impression on me. I connected well with Nilkanta, the little boy who strayed into the home of Kiran and became her favourite. I often felt like Nilkanta. I have honestly lost count of how many times I would have revisited 'Castaway' through these years.

My teacher showed me the power of words.

Wordsworth, Shelley, Keats, and Blake were taught with remarkable aplomb and passion. She led us to the pine forest near the lake for the rehearsals of 'The Bishop's Candlesticks.'

I was given the role of the Bishop. As a youth, I was shy, diffident, and had stage fear but my teacher gently prodded me and encouraged me. She demonstrated and acted out the roles and dialogues. The fun that we had when she was around was immense.

She was exceptionally talented in christening nicknames. 'Kulla Jeeves,' was one among them. Her nicknames were appropriate and humorous. She was a thespian and good in theatrics. She mimicked us and sometimes her colleagues in a light-hearted manner.

How can I ever forget the Karaikudi trip for the KVS Athletic Meet? My teacher escorted the school team and there she was cheering me up all along when I ran my race. During our journey from Ooty, her presence with us was radiant and refreshing. As a child, I always looked out for outdoor activities. I detested the monotony in the classrooms. In the evening that day, as the bus was storming towards Karaikudi, the sun began to dip below the horizon. Suddenly, there was absolute silence and my teacher was engrossed in the spectacular sunset. That day the sunset was particularly a colourful one, with hues of red, orange, and pink streaking across the evening sky. I too gazed at it and experienced the warmth for nature exude from every inch of my body. My teacher's eyes were flooded with tears as she sat in a meditative posture, still lost to the sheer power of this magnificent phenomenon. Every sunset that I get to watch ever since reminds me of my teacher and that wonderful trip. My teacher loved nature; she was awed by the smallest and simplest things, be it a puppy, a kitten, a birdie, or a bud, she treated them with immense devotion and care.

At the athletic meet, I won gold in all three races I ran. My teammates wanted to go for a film. As a child, I detested films and never wanted to accompany them. My teammates hated me for that. I now regret that I shouldn't have been so rigid. Eventually, I had to succumb, but happily slept in the theatre, on a mat I found.

My teacher loved her job and loved her students; she was a teacher by conviction and choice rather than for convenience. Her commitment towards her profession is exemplary. She always believed that a teacher should not be pedestalized, but be accessible. I don't remember a single occasion when she had used the cane, even when corporal punishment was common.

Once she took the extreme risk of taking the entire class on a Sunday to Glenmorgan. That was a memorable trip. We had a whale of a time. We celebrated the freedom and the excitement of being with friends and the great camaraderie that we experienced. My teacher had prepared special food for us, but the next day I was told that she was rebuked by the principal for venturing to do that. She was in tears.

Ramesh, Murali, and I, whom she dubbed as *Tirumurthies* (trifecta), visited her quarters that she shared with two more colleagues. She enlightened us on several issues and broadened our horizons as we sat around her in Gurukul style. Being with children, teaching them, and reaching out to them was not perceived as a cumbersome duty but as a valuable gift that she cherished. For her, teaching was a great act of optimism and art, and she was phenomenal. I remember we had a discussion on J. Krishnamurthy's philosophy. She introduced Linda Goodman, and to this day, I have a personal copy. She was well read, and we were exposed to the writings of the best minds. The meeting always ended with a cup of filtered coffee, the iconic symbol of South India and Tamil culture. The wafting aroma of freshly brewed filter coffee came straight from a stainless-steel tumbler, hand prepared by my teacher. That she served it with love made it further delicious and added a distinct flavour that still lingers with me.

Upon her insistence, once we went to St Stephen's Church on a Sunday morning; my friends also joined us. She was in the church with piety and devotion. She knelt, prayed, and took the blessings. St Stephen's is one of the architectural marvels, with its fabulous stained-glass windows, in a mystical woodland setting. The last supper is another attraction. Even later, a feeling of nostalgia filled me whenever I visited St. Stephens. She practised tolerance and urged us to have a broader outlook, with newer perspectives.

Our holidays were not welcome, as our teacher would leave us for Chennai. How I awaited her letters! She spent hours writing to me, which I truly cherished. I still treasure a bunch of them. How refreshing it was then, as it's now; they are an invaluable gift. Awaiting the postman, the excitement of receiving an inland letter or an envelope addressed by name gave it a personal touch. Reading and re-reading it offered an enthralment that is inexplicable. Her letters were amazing mediums to pour her feelings, share and reciprocate affection, besides educating me on a whole range of issues. Sadly, today letter writing is a lost tradition.

Once on a summer vacation, I found a beautiful card in 'SARAHS Greetings' with a little boy, solitarily standing in a huge, empty stadium, obviously on a desperate wait. The card, I felt evidently reflected my emotional state, and I decided to dash it off to her, which I did. My teacher, from her end, had an interesting story to add, revolving around the card. It seems, when she came across the same card in Chennai, she loved it so much. She wished hard that somebody must send it to her. It would be thrilling indeed, she thought to herself. Good Heavens! She couldn't believe her eyes when my card reached her. She recounted that she jumped and bounced in exhilaration. She narrated this incident to her mom and her mom from then on, added her personal note in the letters that my teacher wrote to me. She was profusely thankful to me. My teacher practised the attitude of gratitude, even for the smallest things. She never hesitated to say 'Thank you' to children. She made it a point to send 'Thank you cards' and 'Thank you notes'. She believed, like Zig Zigler, "The Healthiest of all human emotions is gratitude."

Our course came to an end, and my teacher received her transfer order. We were at crossroads, we went to all our favourite spots once again, to the Pine Forest, to the tiny church that stands alone above the lake. We knew that these were precious moments never to return. I couldn't imagine how much I would be missing my teacher. For the last two years, I had been looking forward every day to learning something new. She turned me around in her own beautiful way. I found my 'Ikigai', my Calling, in one of her sprightly classes. It inspired me to pursue teaching. This was unequivocally clear and there was no turning back.

Interestingly, she never lectured me, never laid down a set of dos and don'ts. Never imposed her beliefs or her persona on me. She won my confidence, bestowed her affection, allowed me to be what I am, and sought to draw the best out of me. She patiently chipped away the rough edges artfully. And when I found her, the miracle had unfolded in those two years of my study under the tutelage of this powerful teacher. Meeting this God-sent angel, I reckon, was a big game changer, a turning point, and a great discovery in my life.

The day of her departure arrived. I was with my two friends, Ramesh and Murali in the Ooty bus stand to see her off. We never spoke, our silence spoke it all. At that tender age, I could never come to terms with this separation. My world had crashed. I began to sulk. The sun went down and darkness engulfed my soul. She gave each of us a five-star chocolate, whose wrapper I've preserved to this day, for four decades.

A childhood poem portrays the melancholy in my heart:

"It's only a nightmare, I thought these days,

That you are leaving this hilly place,

Until the hour came swift to depart.

With laughter and chatter all apart,

I bowed my head broken in heart,

I couldn't pass an hour of that sort,

Far, far from you, I am swooning,

In sorrow, I am sulking."

The conductor blew the whistle. Stealing a final glance at my teacher, through the mist of tears that had clouded our eyes, I reluctantly waved my quivering hands out to her dismal, downcast face; she reciprocated it with her feeble hands.

The whirring and purring engine of the Coimbatore-bound Cheran bus began to thunder and roar until it receded in the hills. Suddenly, life ahead seemed foggy and it took a while for me to totter and move forward.

"No spring, nor summer hath
Such grace as a grandparent."

– John Donne

Behold! What Manner of Love!

This photograph, which I always consider a treasure, is imprinted in my mind, though it was lost after my dad's demise from the family album. It is at least a seventy-year-old picture, or probably even more. It's my grandpa with my mum in his arms. He is immaculately dressed, in a suit and tie. There is an indescribable joy and a father's pride in his smile. He is clean-shaven, sporting a Hitler's moustache, with a gleam on his face.

It is hard to believe that my grandpa was once a young man. Since the time I have seen him, he did not have enough hair on his head, but his visits to the barber never ceased till the end. Somehow, he looked cute after his hairdo and the shower.

There was a gentleness and quietness in the way he conducted himself. His childlike innocence was endearing. He was fair, diminutive, slim, and smart, with a prominent eyebrow and a long and pointed nose.

He was not an extrovert but was committed to daily prayers and devotions. An early bird, he pored over the scriptures, with his thick reading glasses. He highlighted the verses that had appealed to him in red and blue.

Although he had studied only till his standard eight, he could articulate in English with considerable ease. A polyglot in the true sense, he was comfortable with five languages, English, Tamil, Badaga, Kannada, and Malayalam. His father, my great-grandfather was a forester.

Mr. Devaraj Muthappa, my grandpa was a 'field righter' in the Cinchona department, in the pre-independent era. Quinine was extracted from Cinchona, to fight the scourge of malaria. The Nilgiris were found to be ideal for Cinchona plantation and the British Government was keen on it. Mr. Weekly, an Englishman, was director for all the seven divisions and was fond of Grandpa. He took him for his hunting expeditions, fishing, and photography. So, Grandpa had learnt it all.

The home-churned butter, which he smeared with affection, added a special flavour to the bread. No wonder, the bread and bun buttered by Grandpa lent a lovely aroma and distinct taste to it. It still lingers on my tongue. For children like me, that was a thousand times more than a bounty.

Grandpa wasn't cold-blooded but was an expert in roasting country chicken for Christmas. During vacation, we enjoyed the country chicken, desi eggs, fresh milk, ghee, and butter. Grandma used to prepare special ragi rotis and yummy pudding. Grandpa roasted the native potatoes on fire, and munching it, while it was still hot in the winter chillness, was a lifetime experience in itself. He was passionate about farming. He cultivated potatoes, beans, beetroots, and cabbages, which flourished under his lucky hands.

Once in Naduvattam, my mum had taken ill with a serious ailment, and crazy as it may sound, someone suggested black langur meat to be a potent remedy. No hunter was ready to hunt down a monkey. In his desperation to save his daughter, he set all by himself with a gun into the territory of the langurs, knowing well the sensitivity and sacredness of hunting a monkey. The moment they sighted him, with a gun, they grew panicky. They jumped helter-skelter from one tree to the other to flee from the young, determined hunter. But Grandpa was quicker; he targeted one langur and triggered the gun. The bullet had pierced into the ribs. The helpless creature, however, in a bid to save itself, instinctively plucked leaves frantically and stuffed them into its wound to stop the bleeding, but it was of no avail. My mom, it seems, was restored to good health. Word went everywhere about this exotic stuff. People from far and wide had flocked for its medicinal value. Grandpa had narrated this with a sense of remorse and guilt.

Once, Grandpa had sighted a tiger stretching in the afternoon sunlight in a small hillock when he was on his way home during the weekend through the jungle. He just whispered a word of prayer and quietly went his way.

On another occasion, he confronted a porcupine. His Eveready torch, which was always near his bed, had come to his rescue. One Christmas Eve, when the family was awake to usher in Christmas, the whole family heard the movement of the grinding stone at midnight. It was Grandpa who braved to open the door and found a massive bear rocking the millstone. The torch drove the bear to melt in the darkness.

During the day, we meddled with his torch, which did not go well with him. He was possessive about his belongings. He had an antique trunk, which he seldom opened before anyone, and that aroused the curiosity and imagination of his grandchildren. I remember sighting a piece of sandalwood, a box camera, a wristwatch, a few antics, old coins, and black-and-white pictures of his family members intact inside the box.

Come Sundays, he was off to church in his best attire. He had a penchant for suits. His favourite hymn was 'Behold, what manner of love, the father hast bestowed upon us.' His faith in the divine was tremendous… 'The young lions do lack and suffer hunger, but they that wait on the Lord shall not lack any good thing,' was a favourite and oft-quoted verse of his.

Conscious of the transience of life, he would refer to Solomon, 'life is akin to the grass that sprouts in the morn and withers in the evening.'

He was not very learnt but quoted a smatter of Tamil proverbs, shared a few jokes occasionally, and laughed to himself in a typical way when he could not elicit responses from his listeners. Grandma was sarcastic about Grandpa in certain quarters and was fond of snubbing him, but Grandpa brushed it aside and never responded. His unresponsiveness to Grandma was a befitting response by itself.

When he had stayed with us, he was our saviour in readily signing the test papers and test notebooks on behalf of our parents, with a sense of pride. It never occurred to him that we were duping our parents and teachers.

Grandpa detested tamarind and spicy food, which used to aggravate his heart burns. Otherwise, he was not on dieting. He availed free medical service from the dispensary and my mom's employee code no: 1539 worked the magic.

He held Dr. Vishwanathan, the physician, in high esteem whom he used to often consult. A strip of antacids was always with him.

One of the peculiar habits that Grandpa had was taking unduly long hours to finish his meals. He would chew and chew until his mouth used to bulge like a tennis ball, with the lump of food. Granny taunted him for that.

Grandpa was an ardent pet lover and had reared cattle and domesticated hens, cats, and dogs. He loved being with them. The fondest moments with Grandpa were getting into the Shola forest during our annual vacation. While the cattle were left to graze, he would narrate his adventures and tales from his life. He often delighted me with stories from the scripture, with the periodic sound of the turtle dove, and the woodpecker in the backdrop. The eerie silence of the jungle and the flora and the fauna of the Shola grassland, which was home to the birds endemic to the Western Ghats like the black-and-orange flycatcher, the Nilgiri pipit, the Nilgiri laughingthrush, and other species were a common sight.

I have also seen the Nilgiri langur, although I could not trace a tiger or a leopard when we ventured into the Sholas. But we did spot the footprints of boars, deer, leopards, and the Nilgiri tahr. Since my grandparents were living on the fringes of the jungle, they had access to wild meat, and as a child, I tasted many exotic meats.

Once, Judie, our dog, hunted down a young Nilgiri tahr. It was Grandpa's turn to do the rest before this delicacy appeared on our table to whet our appetite.

The sound of the turtle dove makes me nostalgic even today, air dashing me to the years with my grandpa in the Sholas of Doddabetta. The slightly stunted rhododendron trees, in the midst of the thick coarse grass, the flowering sub-alpine shrubs and herbs, mosses, and ferns flash across my mind. A number of grass species, woody climbers, water courses, insects, worms, and beetles unfold before my eyes today.

My brother used to play pranks with our grandparents. Once during our vacation, with our parents off to work, we were left with our grandparents. My brother had locked all the rooms, while we all sat in the hall, which we usually did post lunch. He asked Grandpa, "Why did you choose to marry a *karvachi* (darkling) being a handsome guy?" Grandpa rebuked him silently. "Why do you want to rake up old issues?" Grandma was evidently embarrassed and wanted to leave the place, but all doors were bolted. However, as children, we had great fun watching their reactions. They were lovely folks and we loved them more than our parents.

It seems, Mr. Weekly offered to take Grandpa to England when he had left India but Grandpa's elder sister Julie declined the offer. Grandpa's life would have taken unimaginable turns with several possibilities had he left for England in those days.

After my education, I left home to pursue my career. I had always missed my grandpa. I used to send pocket money to him, which he faithfully acknowledged. It was thrilling to receive those short letters, handwritten by him. I cherish them to this day. Whenever I visited my home, I found him fit and healthy as ever. He would walk miles upon miles even at that age. He was not the kind of person who used to get confined to home, nor did he allow the spirit of infirmity to creep into his body. He wasn't fussy about his advancing age, either. Grandma used to remark, "He is a man always with a wheel on his feet."

Once in the mid-90s, I was journeying from Belgaum to Hyderabad on official work. In my itinerary, I had planned to visit my hometown after the completion of my work. I had meticulously packed the 'dream suit,' that I had intended to gift my grandpa on his birthday. I knew he would love it and had already envisioned my grandpa with the suit. The royal blue fabric I had chosen was versatile, and a gift from his grandson was going to impact him much. I was more than eager to savour his reactions, and also celebrate him with his new attire.

That night was a turbulent night; while all my co-passengers were heavily snoring, I was 'twisting and turning,' and I knew intuitively all was not well. I couldn't get even a wink of sleep, but I could never figure out what had happened.

Early in the morn, when I had called up home in anxiety, my dad broke the news that 'Grandpa is no more.' It was sudden and peaceful. In the telephone booth in Hyderabad, the moist imprint of the last physical touch, a gentle forehead kiss of my beloved grandpa, played on me and held its grip on me for many days to come.

The idea of Grandpa's dream suit lay in smithereens.

Coincidentally, it seems Grandpa's younger brother, Mr. George Gideon had come on a visit from Bangalore the same night. "He drank the last cup of Horlicks from my hand. Your grandpa's face had suddenly illumined when he saw me. It's the Lord's doing." He told me later when I had met him.

I sadly missed the funeral, as I was stranded in Hyderabad. Oh! How my heart pined to be there. It seems all sang his favourite hymn, "Behold, What manner of love," while he lay in peace, with his face aglow.

That destiny had deprived me of presenting 'my dream suit' and the fact that I missed his funeral weighed on me. I also suffered from 'non-closure of emotions'. After several decades, I took my family to show the little farmhouse where my grandparents had lived in Doddabetta. I went there in search of my beloved grandpa and catch up with my precious childhood.

Not many days after his demise, my grandpa appeared to me in a glorious dream, with his signature smile and astoundingly clad in the very same dream suit and a Bible in his hand. His eyes glinted and he had dazzled with it. He remained silent all through, but his gazes were cascading with love and gratitude. It was so realistic, and ever since that dream, peace had reigned in my heart.

By now a certain sacredness and a sentiment had surrounded the 'dream suit.' It became a treasure. A few days after that special dream, propelled by a sudden fit of fancy and curiosity, I opened my wardrobe to feel my grandpa's dream suit. I rummaged through the wardrobe and to my utter shock, I found it missing. I knew for certain that no human could lay hands on it. But then, how did it suddenly disappear? It remains a mystery.

Behold! What manner of love!

"There is always some
madness in love,
But there is also always
Some reason in madness."

– Fredrick Nietzsche

I Can't Stop Loving You

Uncle William, as he was fondly called, was well over sixty, short in stature, fair, and handsome. He wore his favourite half-sleeved white, cotton shirt. His silvery hair and sideburns were in sync with his thick eyebrows. His hands quivered while he made the receipts of the hostel and mess bill in Selaiyur Hall in M.C.C. Tambaram. But his writing showed no resemblance of his senility, while his thick glasses revealed, it though. His feet wobbled and he found it difficult to climb or alight the stairs to his room. There was a certain glow in his eyes that only betrayed the gloom that lay shelved in his inner self. No wonder he was sometimes grumpy. However, all the boys in Selaiyur had a certain fondness for him.

One evening, Tippu my friend who was close to Uncle William, took me to his room in Selaiyur Hall. A sparklingly clean room with scarce furniture, that a bachelor required, with an Onida TV and a tape recorder awaited us. The old love songs of the baritone Jim Reeves were softly playing out like a brook brewing from a fairyland.

Uncle served us with an aromatic coffee and ginger biscuits, which pleased us. "Uncle, Prem is from the Nilgiris," said Tippu. "Do you know it was my dream to honeymoon in the Nilgiris," Uncle stated. Tippu and I exchanged glances, a little embarrassed. That Uncle was once a youth was simply unacceptable to us.

Uncle William was a Tamil movie buff of the 80s, and he discussed them at length, but neither of us could relate to it.

Strangely, all the while I had an eerie feeling, of another person cohabiting the room, though I knew he was a bachelor and staying alone. Soon, a black-and-white picture became very compelling. It was in a grainy, wooden frame with decorative edging, setting the picture apart from its surroundings. It was stately and was integrated into the frame and the wall. There was something sentimental, featuring a girl of about eighteen years, gorgeously draped in a half-saree, with her tresses dazzling, with a bunch of jasmine. The summer sun glinted on her comely face. A few strands of her locks loosely played on her cheeks, which lent an inexplicable charm. Her well-marked brows joined the narrow bridge of her long and pointed nose. Upon enquiry, Uncle declared that it was his sweetheart. "Look," he said with a fire aglow in his eyes. "Those jasmines were knitted on her hair with my own hands. I had nurtured them for her." He added, "This picture was shot by me at Marina Beach, on a sunny, breezy afternoon. We walked alongside its sandy shores and had a long walk. Too often, we had the sea to ourselves. We collected the shells and sauntered from St. George to Beasant Nagar spanning about 13 km."

"Those days," Uncle persisted, "the Marina was much cleaner and safer." When we raised our eyebrows, Uncle taking notice of it retorted, "True love never counts time and distance." "We sang together gleefully," he continued, "shouted 'I love you' at the top of our voice." Ramola read her poems celebrating our love. She was a budding but brilliant poet. Every adventure, every experience, every emotion, she skilfully weaved into a beautiful poem. Uncle quickly ushered in a file that showcased the treasury of hundreds of poems, handwritten by Ramola. "Even after decades, her words are uplifting and music to my soul. I religiously meditate on them every day."

Uncle was in no mood to stop, he went on to vent out. "Once we launched a beautiful kite. Ramola designed and crafted kites with great attention to symmetry, accuracy, and beauty. Her kites hit the skies with ease, achieving the highest flight standards. Kite flying was transformative and we enjoyed piloting the kite together. We felt that we were paragliding at that moment." Uncle was caught up in a train of such memories. His face illumined and was endued with a mysterious power. He was akin to a baby whose face beamed at the sight of a fluttering butterfly. "She was the leader of our team and was fiercely possessive about me. She was a tomboy at heart and would run, romp, and climb the trees. She would shove me into the water, brave the waves and play pranks with me."

"She would never retreat from fighting injustice, be it the auto driver, her teacher, or anyone. Ramola was a sensation, but she loved her freedom and loved me greatly. She had unique tastes and wanted to live every inch of her life. We dreamt about our future life together. We wanted to travel and explore the world. Ramola had a penchant for horse riding, kite flying, paragliding, and rafting. We had together designed a vision board about almost everything that we will be doing together." Interestingly, Uncle showed us the sketch of the future cottage that she had designed in Siargao Islands in the Philippines amidst the pristine white beaches, coconut woodlands, and emerald mangrove forests. She had christened the cottage as '*Wiliola*'. That was amazingly romantic. Tippu abruptly stopped Uncle at this juncture and dared to ask him, "Uncle, where is Ramola now? What happened between you and her?" There was a sudden silence in the room. Uncle was jolted to reality by this question. Gradually, he regained his composure, and with a deep sigh, said, "The last trip of ours was to the beach near the famous Mahabalipuram. Ramola was buoyant and bubbly that day, with a pink skirt and fresh blossoms of jasmine on her cascading hair. That evening we returned to our homes and tragically that day happened to be the last day of our tryst. It's almost five decades and I am still on my wait for her."

Uncle's voice choked. "My Ramola mysteriously went missing, never to return. All my efforts to trace her whereabouts proved futile. I searched for her in her neighbourhood, night and day. I waited near her college, lingered near her church on Sundays, and enquired friends and neighbours, but didn't get a clue. Some said her father was under orders of a sudden transfer, while others maintained that her father was on punishment, and they had to leave the city overnight. But why didn't she reach out to me? Couldn't she inform me? Could she not have posted an inland letter? How could be silent and cold for all these years?" Uncle William lamented, "I have no answer. It remains a mystery to be resolved. Would she be on an exotic island rafting and riding horses? Would she be wandering in her favourite Bamboo Forest in Japan? Or perhaps she might be on Easter Island in Chile. These were her dream places. But I am certain, she wouldn't have ventured without me. I am awaiting her arrival and I live each day feasting on the dreams of yesteryears. I can't stop loving her."

The tape had ushered the song – 'I can't stop loving you' resonating the same sentiments drifting in the air. The drizzle outside lifted the aroma of the gulmohars in the campus and sprinkled in the air with a sudden gush of wind; Crimson Rose, a gorgeous butterfly had fluttered inside the room from the portico. It had perched on the shoulders of Uncle William for a few fleeting moments and flitted away deep into the woods.

Reclining in a cane chair, Uncle William floated in rhythm with the song 'I can't stop loving you' with the same glow in his eyes. Although he lay twisted and gnarled like an old banyan tree, that was perhaps the last time I saw Uncle William. But that evening remained with me.

At that instance, Tippu and I felt like being ruthlessly knocked down into the valley from the mountaintop after an adventurous ascent. It was difficult for us to get reconciled with Uncle's tragic tale of woe.

Our memorable two-year stint in M.C.C. suddenly came to a close, and we were scattered all across the globe. Tippu went overseas. Whenever he was in India, we used to speak to each other. Each of us found ourselves busy, chasing after our passion and making something out of our lives.

After almost two decades and more, I was once in Kilpauk Cemetery, Chennai, to attend the funeral of Wesley, another friend of mine from M.C.C. He was a pastor in North America and had collapsed with a brain haemorrhage. It was shocking to see a lifeless Wesley, a 'happy-go-lucky guy' lying there in the coffin. It was hard to come to terms with his untimely demise. After the funeral service, I took my usual stroll inside the cemetery. I do this whenever I get a chance. I have a penchant for engaging with the epitaphs engraved on the tombs. I try to get to know the folks who had gone to their Maker and what they stood for. An epitaph is a celebration of the deceased, their philosophy, and their legacy. I also get to read the text from the scriptures engraved on the tombs. I often remember the epitaph of Khushwant Singh that he wrote for himself:

'Here lies one who spared neither man nor God; Waste not your tears on him, he was a sod; Writing nasty things he regarded as great fun; Thank the Lord he is dead, this son of a gun.'

For me, walking through a cemetery is a humble experience and rubbing shoulders with the reality of death. Some tombstones were stately, some were austerely simple.

The cemetery at Kilpauk was weighed down by space crunch and badly maintained. I found most graves covered with bushes and creepers, the dense growth of which made it difficult to reach. As I was walking past and observing each tomb, I was drawn to a particular cemetery, which seemed to be well-maintained, standing out, with a bunch of fresh fragrant jasmines sparkling on the tomb. I could not but stop when I read the epitaph, a sudden spark ignited my mind and it raced me way back to my M.C.C. days. It was engraved:

'I can't stop loving you'

Mr. William

D.O.B – 07.01.1930

D.O.D – 18.05.2019

Immediately, I called up Tippu to confirm whether it was the same Uncle William of the old. Tippu gave the confirmation and said, "Uncle had passed away two years ago and he was buried in the cemetery at Kilpauk." I stood there in silence and recalled that evening in his room. The entire thing unfolded before me and I relived that evening.

Now I was wondering regarding the fresh jasmines. Out of sheer curiosity, I enquired the grave keeper, who told me that an elderly woman has been visiting the grave regularly for the past two years. She has been tending the grave and has been offering flowers. Before I left, I tipped the grave keeper to get some information about the person. Within a week, he promptly called me to inform me that the woman's name is Ramola. I could not believe my ears, though that's what I was eager to hear. Ramola, Uncle William's sweetheart, still in love.

Now I am eagerly awaiting to make a trip soon to the Kilpauk Cemetery in Chennai, only to meet Aunt Ramola and get to hear her side of the story.

'I can't stop loving you.'

"But perhaps the most important lesson I learnt is that there are no walls between humans and the elephants except those that we put up ourselves."

– Lawrence Anthony

The Call from The Wild

An elephant evokes unparalleled sensations in me. Is it the deft craftsmanship and mastery of this magnificent creature? Or simply the spectacle of its humungous stature? Perhaps the numerous elephant snapshots my grandma had recounted in her exceptional style had left an indelible impression on me.

My great-grandfather, I believe, was a forester and had many precarious encounters with elephants. Once on an evening during his customary rounds, being attacked by an elephant, he ran for his life into a small bridge. He sat crouched and cowered watching the monstrous feet. The wild elephant evidently could not reach him but was determined to confront my great-grandfather and played several tricks to bring him out of his hideout. Initially, the animal feigned absolute silence to dupe him into thinking that the creature had left. When that did not work in its favour, the animal sucked and hurled water inside vehemently, in a bid to flush him out from the bridge. The drama persisted till dawn and he had a providential escape with the appearance of the milkman that drove the elephant into the jungle.

On another occasion, a tribal was intimidated by an elephant and he dodged it by running around the bamboo shrubs. Eventually, he climbed up a tree adroitly only to discover the animal shaking the branches with its mighty trunk. The panic-stricken victim leapt from one tree to another. These and other anecdotes enhanced my penchant for the pachyderm. Not surprisingly, many elephant dreams have haunted me. I fondly remember watching the 'King Elephant' movie with my whole school at Ooty.

A few scenes of a Tamil film, 'Ram, Lakshman' (1981), starring Kamala Hassan and Sri Priya, were shot in my school, featuring Lakshman, an elephant. With trepidation in my heart, I reached out and my quivering fingers felt the thick skin of Lakshman. That was the first time I ever touched an elephant: the sensation still lingers with me.

Once in Mudumalai Sanctuary, in a good gesture, a wild elephant waited and let me pass by, before crossing the road, like a moving mountain.

My days in Assam offered enchanting elephant experiences. It was fabulous to wade through the towering wild grasses in Kaziranga on Elephant Safari into the territory of the one-horned rhino.

On my birthday, I was traversing through the Kaziranga National Park from Jorhat on a dusty and deserted road during the evening, desperately missing the customary wishes. But a pleasant surprise awaited me. I had spotted a massive tusker. Swiftly, I alighted from the vehicle and gazed at this incredible creature, majestically posing to me without a stir. The evening was electrified by its mystical presence, at least to me.

I lost count of time until the forest guards cautioned me to proceed. Bidding adieu to this 'wild wonder,' I left enriched and enthralled. As I regained my composure, a still small voice whispered loud and clear, 'That was your birthday gift.' I thanked God profusely for that visual bonanza and inestimable gift, which will linger with me for a lifetime.

Destiny had for eight years relocated me to Shimoga, and I lived in the proximity of an elephant camp in Gajanur, the land of the elephants. Interestingly, I never looked for bridges to hide but was engaged with this enigmatic and gentle colossus. I frequented them often, in Sakrebyle Elephant Camp, which is located on the Shimoga-Mangalore highway, near the backwaters of the Tunga River.

Surrounded by Shettihalli Wildlife Sanctuary, this camp is a bustling rescue, rehabilitation, and training centre, along with an eco-tourism zone.

I was privileged to watch the spectacular giants living life to the full: feasting, wallowing in the waters, and making merry against the picturesque background of the hills. Elephants love water and the mahouts bathing them and scrubbing their bodies was a lifetime experience. I have participated in this ritual numerous times, and I always felt rejuvenated. Being in their world was awesome. I freely touched them, felt their touch, fed them with the feed that the mahouts prepared, and held their trunks whenever they gently laid them on my head to enthuse me. I felt blessed.

I began to understand their family structure, social intelligence, communication, and the remarkable leadership of the matriarch. I was always super delighted to watch the elephant calves. They were cute, with their glowing wrinkly skin, their adorable curled-up little trunks, and their playing, learning, and bonding with their families. The extraordinary care shown by their grandmas and family members is always amazing.

I befriended the mahouts and gathered a fund of information from them. Their first-hand experience, expertise, and valuable insights into elephants were encyclopaedic. Mr. Jalil Ahmed, the chief mahout, in an open interview, enlightened my students about elephants in our school.

I have listened to innumerable spine-chilling stories from the mahouts. Once, on Elephant Day, all the mahouts of the camp were invited and were specially felicitated. The mahouts were thrilled and moved to tears by the honour that our institution had bestowed upon them.

When I was in Gajanur, the land of the elephants, one midnight, I received a surprise invitation to watch a wild elephant being brought into the camp. This particular elephant had gone berserk and killed a few folks in the neighbouring district. It was captured and translocated to the Sakrebyle Elephant Camp for rehabilitation. I rushed to the training centre and watched the whole operation unfold, live before my eyes, at midnight.

The operation lasted for more than four hours with Kumki elephants joining forces. Kumki elephants were trained to capture and tame wild elephants. The captured wild elephant was transported in a huge truck, completely chained, with its legs fastened to huge ropes.

Now the first challenge was to dismount the animal from the truck and then thrust it into the *Kraal* (enclosure), which would be its home for the next year. The *Kraal* is a pen to confine rogue elephants, constructed by the tamed elephants in Sakrebyle with solid eucalyptus logs.

The wild elephant refused to budge and put up stiff resistance. Its aggressiveness and anger were evident in its looks and body movements, although it was in chains. However, the Kumki elephants, by their remarkable training experience and timely action, worked in tandem with their mahouts to subdue the rogue elephant. It was a moment of triumph, a nail-biting finish, and a heave of relief when the giant was put behind bars; but at the same time, it was sad to watch this wild jewel in captivity.

Two mahouts were placed in charge of the captive animal. I often visited these mahouts to encourage them and also out of sheer curiosity to get to watch how they handled the animal.

In the initial days, the mahouts had a hard-hitting time. It was sleepless nights, hard labour, patience, and terror. There was no end to its rebellion and aggression.

The captured elephant would want to tear down the structure. It would move in reverse motion and bang the *Kraal*. It would start digging into the *Kraal* and would make attempts to climb over the enclosure.

One day, when the mahout was seated just outside the *Kraal*, suddenly the elephant flung a bamboo stick targeting him. The bamboo stick came speeding like an arrow and just grazed him. That was a narrow escape. He stood massive like a mountain and his rage erupted like a volcano.

For the mahouts, there was no option. It was a duty they were obliged to shoulder. A gargantuan challenge to calm the elephant, win its confidence, treat its wounds, feed him to satisfy his enormous appetite, clean the *Kraal*, and train the elephant.

Late in the evenings, the mahouts would strike up a conversation with the animal. It was a one-to-one communication. Mahouts in Sakrebyle Elephant Camp spoke a mix of languages that included Hindi, Bengali, Urdu, and Kannada. And the elephants took their cues from it.

"Hey, I will take care of you… Calm down… Don't worry… I will feed you… I am there for you…"

This communication went on for days and months. By making appropriate adjustments to the *Kraal*, which restricted the movements of the animal, the elephants would be scrubbed, cleaned, and treated.

The mahouts offered sugar cane, jaggery, straw, with rice, salt, and coconut in paddy straw, after each personal session of endearment with the animal in distress.

The method used for training the animal is human positive reinforcement, an immediate reward-based training.

Surprisingly, after consistent efforts of the mahouts, the animal calmed down, rehabilitated, obeyed the commands, and developed a rapport with the mahouts.

In less than one year, on an appointed day, in the presence of officials, it was eventually released from the *Kraal*. I was present there to watch the whole process. I felt that the animal looked emaciated, but it was calm. As an educationist I used to wonder, even after years of training, sometimes a child is not trained and transformed. Of course, it's erroneous to compare an animal with a child in school. But then the takeaway for me was 'care,' 'communication,' 'personal touch,' and 'rigorous training.'

In Sri Lanka, in Pinnawala Elephant's Orphanage, one of its kind, I had the most amazing time during a fruit-feeding event. I could touch the pachyderms. I sat there for what seemed like hours, engrossed in watching these creatures bathing in the Pinnawala River.

A few years ago, I was on a visit to JNV Chamarajanagar. It was my birthday, with no wishes reaching me due to network issues as the school was remotely tucked away in the jungles of Honderbalu. Just as the appearance of a colossal tusker in the Kaziranga National Park had appeased me, I wished for a revisitation of that visual treat, knowing well that BR Hills in Chamarajanagar are rich with wildlife and populous with pachyderms. With great expectations, I climbed the hills. I was all eyes and ears, lingering and waiting for the momentous occasion. To my utter disappointment, the miracle did not occur as I wished it to happen. I noticed mounds of elephant dung everywhere, but the animal I most craved for, remained elusive. Instead, a deer appeared to me. I returned to JNV with hopes crashed to smithereens.

It was time for lunch and Mr. Daniel, the Principal of JNV Chamarajanagar, accompanied me to the dining hall. While on our way, from nowhere, suddenly a huge trumpeting thundered from the hills of the forest ranges. For a split second, we were stupefied. With bated breath, I lifted my eyes aloft to the hills, evidently searching for the animal in excitement and curiosity. But again, the animal remained elusive and not visible. Mr. Daniel confessed that in all five years of his stay there, he never got to hear a trumpeting of this magnitude. Instinctively, that call, I knew, was not merely a beautiful coincidence, but was exclusively meant for me. This time it was an aural treat. Nature has its distinct ways. I thanked the Lord for yet another special greeting and gift, proffered by the pachyderm. The call from the wild!

"I walk this empty street
On the boulevard of broken dreams."

– Green Day

The Anklet Dreamer

Far away in Lakhargaon, in a small Assamese village, was an isolated old bamboo hut. A broken fence with thorny hedges separated it from the dusty road. A huge bamboo shrub provided a canopy of cover to the hut. Not far away a gulmohar tree adorned the corner of the road.

It was early morning and the skies were clear. The faint cries of the morning train that had pulled off from Moirabari junction, shambling its way to Nagaon, disturbed young Swapna, who was in the hut. She woke up. In her reluctance to dispense with slumber, she continued to lie down and recalled the dream that paraded before her.

The hoots of the owl and the howls of the jackals did not perturb her fantasy. To her, it was a jubilant night. She was decked up in the best of her attire. Her dreams had given her wings and she was joyfully riding on it. Her eyes were sparkling with ecstasy as she envisioned herself playing with a silvery ball.

But the dawn had trampled her rosy dreams.

She mumbled, "I wish the night had continued." What good can this new day usher, to this ugly duckling of despair?"

She wiped her eyes, yawned, stretched her hands, and felt the pangs of the passing dream. She desperately wanted to cleave to it, but it vanished in thin air. She reluctantly got out of her bed. The nauseating stench of the pigs and the odour of the cow dung were thick in the air, but Swapna had become immune to it.

The wind quietly played with her clumsy hair. On the other side of the road, she noticed students of the boarding school performing their physical exercises. The teachers were rigorously training them. 'Oh, how fortunate those children are,' she muttered to herself. 'Would I find myself there at least in my next birth?'

Swapna, clad in a yellow wrinkled middy, moved to the backyard of her hut and surveyed those vast stretches of paddy fields. This was her daily practice.

As she stood there silently nursing her grief, she heard the pleasant cooing of birds and soon spotted a pair of turtle doves gliding gleefully and darting from one tree to another and eventually alighting on an electric line. While she was still engrossed with the winged wonders, jostling in each other's company, she abruptly heard a spark and in the spur of the moment, one of the turtle doves crumbled and crashed into the paddy fields. Swapna sprang like a deer to the spot and picked up its lifeless body. She noticed a spot of blood and guessed it was electrocuted. Her heart was thumping faster. She held the cute little thing fondly to her breasts and noticed the other pair curiously surveying its mate from above. Swapna could never come to terms with such a close encounter with death. She stood there dumbstruck and mused about the evanescence of life.

She looked above empathetically at the bereaved bird. At this moment, she became oblivious to her own predicament and lamented at the untimely death of its pair.

Swapna was a fourteen-year-old, wheatish, short-statured, Assamese girl, with small eyes, a round face and short curly hair. She was habitually shy. She was an introvert and a solitary child. She found comradeship in *Kalu* and *Bholi*, her canine pets. These country dogs brought a therapeutic touch to her. She shared her little rice and dal with her companions.

She had dreamy eyes and seldom smiled, but whenever she did, she beamed like the sudden flash of sunlight. Always there was a pall of gloom covering her otherwise pretty countenance.

Her widowed mother Jonali was a daily wager in the boarding school and Swapna did a housemaid's job on the same campus. Swapna lost her father when she was still a toddler and had absolutely no memory of him. Her mom stopped her from attending school when the expenses of her books and uniform started pinching her purse.

Every day, she lazily did the household chores. It sounded pleasant when she addressed her South Indian mistress as '*didi*'. She slowed down her work when she saw the girl students walking past her and her eyes pursued long after them until they disappeared into the school. She was very curious to learn English. 'Would I ever be able to articulate in English so elegantly,' she often thought when she heard the students speak.

When the mistress parted with her dresses to Swapna in a bid to clear the old stock from her wardrobe, Jonali altered them to fit Swapna. Each time she wore them, she became chirpy and confident. She glittered like the newly blossomed petunias and volunteered to the market for shopping with her mom.

During the day, Swapna spent her time covering the bamboo walls with muddy paste in order to fill the gaps to prevent the peering looks of peeping Toms and also to keep the hut cool from the scorching summer heat.

The hut could only boast of broken fibre chairs, a make-shift cot prepared by Bipul, her step-father, a few vessels, a handful of clothes, a plastic pot, a broken mirror, an old transistor, a *Jappi* and *Sorai* and nothing more. But it was spick and span. The door proudly displayed a beautiful curtain that the mistress had given.

Assam witnessed torrential rains with thunder and lightning and floods always unleashed havoc. During such times, the family were worried, praying hard that their hut should not be swept away. She took care of the pigs that grunted for food. The pigs were left in their care by the owner of the hut for which they were paid a paltry sum from the sale after the litter. She also reared the calf which was their only wealth. She waited each day for the hens to lay eggs. If she is a little careless, the cat might gobble it or the hungry urchins may steal it.

She craved *Maas* (fish) like every Assamese, but her family couldn't afford it for her. Each time the vendors passed by with the freshwater fish from the Brahmaputra in huge vessels neatly placed and tied on the cycle carriers, her mouth watered. In her leisure time, whenever the batteries of the transistor permitted her, she listened to the vibrant songs of Zubeen and connected with the melancholic melodies of Bhupen Hazarika, the legendary Assamese singer. Swapna also tuned her ears to the plaintive notes of the flute that floated in the air. It synchronized with her feelings and touched the inner recesses of her being.

The rustle of the bamboo leaves, the myriad species of birds that hopped in ecstasy, the paddy fields carpeted miles upon miles, the red hibiscus that greeted her every day, the potted plants in the sprawling campus of the boarding school, the bottle palm, the picas, the Ashoka trees in rows, the exquisite flowers, the gorgeous orchids, the mighty Brahmaputra, the virgin air that she was breathing, she connected with all these bounties of nature. It was part of her daily existence.

During festive seasons, she gazed at the girls who were clad in their Mekhela, the beautiful traditional Assamese wear. How she wished to join them in the Bihu dances! When the girls of the school performed '*Sathriya,*' the classical dance, she watched with a delightful eagerness. She regretted, 'Destiny has not carved me out for these simple pleasures.' She also missed the Bihu delicacies.

But Swapna had only one absorbing passion and that was to own and adorn a pair of silvery anklets. She dreamt about it night and day. She saw the anklets everywhere. She saw it in the clouds. She imagined it materializing to her in an unusual and magical manner. She believed the anklets would transfigure her into an angel in a twinkling of an eye and redeem all that she lost as a child.

Days lapsed into weeks and weeks turned into months and her anklet dreams were growing larger and irresistible. She shared her desires with her mother. "Ma, I can't afford this dream to elude me as others have. I wanted to attend school, I wanted to dance, I loved gaudy dresses, I had dreamt of becoming a poet, and now all is lost, my dad too has gone. Please, please, Ma." She implored her mother, falling at her feet and sobbing with tears, "I swear I don't want anything else." Jonali sensed every pore of her daughter oozing with passion.

She was silent. She never wanted to turn down the genuine pleas of her daughter, but at the same time, where would she cough up the money from? Even if she dares to purchase the anklets, how would she feed the family? Bipul her husband, whom she presently lived with, after she lost her first husband, seldom got any work to do with no factories around. They were also landless. Even if he earns, he drinks, falling into bad company. Jonali joined a paper mill after her widowhood and met Bipul there. She wanted a companion and chose to live with him. Their relationship was consummated and a baby boy was born. Consequently, Jonali underwent a tubectomy and unfortunately, the baby succumbed to a dreadful fever due to want of treatment and the lackadaisical attitude of the medical personnel in the government hospital.

Bipul was disappointed that he had no progeny of his own. Jonali was anxious about whether Bipul would abandon her to remarry. A couple of times, Jonali sought the advice of the mistress if there was any possibility to conceive again and bear children.

Jonali requested the mistress the next day for a loan of thousand rupees. Jonali was earlier doing the household chores in the house of the mistress. She had the habit of borrowing loans and later adjusted them with her monthly wages. But her mistress counselled her not to take loans for such luxuries. Jonali tried but couldn't persuade her mistress.

The next day, the mistress suggested Swapna to not squander away the hard-earned money of her mother. "Didi… I just like them," quivered Swapna.

Her hopes were shattered. She started sulking. She sighed and mourned, "Why am I so awfully poor and should poverty stifle my small wishes?" She sat reclining on the wobbling walls of her hut. Her two hungry pets were lying beside her. While *Bholi* licked Swapna's feet, *Kalu* crouched and gazed into her drenched eyes buried in her sorrow. She sat there for what seemed like hours with her pets until her mother took her inside.

Jonali spoke to her but Swapna was furious and emotional. "You take away all that I earn and leave nothing to me," she yelled out at her mom apparently in her dejected state. Jonali tended the fire and prepared red tea for her daughter, patted her, and gave her biscuits that she had pilfered from the school kitchen stores.

Then quickly Jonali went to her sister who lived close by in the village and pleaded to lend a thousand rupees. But her sister wouldn't budge as she resented the idea of a jewel. She advised Jonali, "You better repair your hut before the onset of monsoon lest you be washed away by the floods. What is so urgent about anklets?" She sarcastically retorted, "Is your daughter a princess?"

Soon the anklets kicked up a controversy and triggered a fusillade of ridicule. It was good material for gossip among the village women. The women were seething in envy at the prospect of Swapna wearing them. They detested Jonali as she was illegally living with Bipul. "She is characterless and should be ostracized from this village," said one of the women disdainfully. "Yes, she is shameless and is a disgrace to all the women folk of this village," added another one with contempt.

They were already jealous that she managed to get a job for a thousand rupees in the boarding school.

With nowhere to go and none to show an iota of mercy, she returned home only to find Bipul in an inebriated state and hurling abuses at her. "What kind of a woman are you? Can't you give me a son? Leave me for good, you creature of mischance."

That night she couldn't get a wink of sleep. She was exploring all possibilities to raise money for her daughter's anklet. Her only possession was the calf that she had purchased after penny-pinching for several years. She decided to sell it. Word went around in the village and prospective buyers lined up to examine the calf. She sold it for three thousand rupees and took fifty per cent advance immediately.

The same evening, she took her daughter to the local market and purchased her dream object, a beautiful pair of silver anklets. Swapna hugged her mom and kissed her profusely. Her excitement knew no bounds. She wore it and jumped for joy. "*Suwali* (girl), it's enough for me that you are happy," Jonali exclaimed.

But the man who had purchased the calf was absconding.

The news of the purchase was concealed from the mistress. Swapna was very proud of her prized possession. She becomes the cynosure of the eyes of the women and the young girls in the village: a small heroine in the village. The mother and daughter visited the *Namghar* and Bardowa, the birthplace of Mahapurush Sankardev (the Vaishnavite saint). The anklets were held in reverence and became a sacrosanct object to the whole family. She lived each day with a glow of happiness and a sense of accomplishment.

Barely a few weeks later, a thief broke into their hut and Swapna's prized possession was stolen. It was difficult for Swapna to digest this sudden loss. She could hardly come to terms with the bitter truth. Jonali and Bipul launched a massive hunt for the lost treasure.

One day in the local market, two youths were selling a silver ball. They demanded four hundred rupees from the shopkeeper. When the deal was struck, a local cop appeared and noticed the incident. He smelt something fishy and intervened and interrogated the youth, "What do you do?"

"Nothing, we are unemployed," replied the youth arrogantly. Upon further enquiry, they confessed that they had stolen from Lakhargaon and melted it. "Why did you indulge in this theft?" questioned the cop. "No jobs, no money, hunger, starvation," quickly came the reply, with no sense of remorse.

Swapna lay devastated. Her hopes were broken to smithereens. She burst into tears and turned hysterical. She was inconsolable. "Oh God, this is too much… too much… it's better you kill us," Jonali screamed and cried bitterly. Bipul in a fit of anger thrashed both of them.

The village women secretly rejoiced at the turn of events and found peace in what they thought was retributive justice. "We had cautioned them… they deserved it… God has taught them a good lesson," they stated with a note of triumph.

When the family knew that it was in the custody of the cop, they had a flicker of hope that he would dutifully return the silver ball.

Swapna's tantalizing hopes soared up and down and the anklet-ache pressed her hard.

But the day never dawned when the silver ball ever bounced in her life.

"The train is a small world moving through a larger world."

– Elisha Cooper

In Brahmaputra Mail

After what seemed a long wait, eventually the Delhi–Dibrugarh bound Brahmaputra Mail entered Chaparmukh station in Assam. After an estimated sixty-two stops, during its course through various stations, the train was abysmally late by more than three hours.

I hurriedly boarded the train into the AC coach, took my seat with a heave of relief, quickly surveyed the cabin, and glanced at my co-travellers. The wheels of the train fell in rhythm with the tracks. The sound of the fans emitted a distinct kind of music.

In the upper berth, opposite my seat, a young mother was absorbed cuddling her child. In turn, the child reciprocated, pedalling his little feet, with peals of laughter and giggles. Both the window seats were comfortably occupied by a family with a grown-up daughter. The middle-aged man was well-built, clean-shaven, fair, and bespectacled with his friendly overtures. He was generously buying snacks for all in the cabin from the vendors, bread omelette, pakora, vada etc. We exchanged smiles but did not converse as yet. His wife and daughter acknowledged my presence but were shy to talk to me. The young mother in the upper berth was busily feeding the little child with bits and pieces of the snacks. She greeted me with a sunny smile. Her skin was yellowish with a brown tinge, and her hair was black; she had a prominent cheekbone. Her lips were thick, but her eyes were dark and small.

After a while, she initiated, "Sir, it looks like you are from South India." I responded, "Yes."

Then in a bid to continue the conversation, she asked me, "Sir, where are you going? What is your occupation?"

I replied, "I am invited as a guest speaker in Dibrugarh and working as a principal in JNV, a boarding school run by the Union Govt." She was happy to introduce herself as a teacher. She continued to cuddle and play with her child. It was a pleasure to watch the real and purest bond between a mother and a child. She was incredibly proud of her motherhood. The child was a world unto her, and for the little fellow, his mom was his everything.

Now the bespectacled gentleman broke his silence. Perhaps to win me over, he stated, "Sir, I had toured South India extensively and was impressed with Meenakshi Temple, Rameshwaram, and the pristine beauty of Kerala, and the famous and ancient Sharadamba Temple in Sringeri in Karnataka." He dwelt at length to describe his positive observations of Chennai, Hyderabad, and Bangalore.

Upon enquiry, he divulged that he was an employee in Digboi, the oil city of Assam, where the first oil well in Asia was drilled. His wife was quiet, seemingly self-conscious but her eyes and ears were tuned to what we were conversing. She was strikingly pretty with her nose stud perfectly in place, which added a stunning elegance to her face. The young girl, evidently their daughter, was grumpy, unlike her parents. She was restless and showed no interest in our conversation. We discussed our jobs and life in general in the North East.

"What is the next station?" I curiously asked him. He promptly answered, "Lumding." The name seemed strange, so I asked him twice to repeat Lumding. "Lumding is one of the oldest railway stations in India, with a huge junction," he added. The town is the gateway to the enchanting Lumding–Badarpur hill tract and connects upper Assam. I was pleased to get all this information, unasked. As I peeped out from the speeding train, the hilly landscape with dense forests offered a visual treat.

The young girl was cleaving and clinching to her mother. She was mumbling and whispering something into the ears of her mum. Daughters have an extraordinary claim and connect with their moms. She would be hardly in her 20s, quite well-built, round, and chubby-faced. Her skin had a glow, and her hair was straight but unkempt owing to the journey. Her tiny, weary eyes welled with tears and her lips were dry. I knew all was not well with her and her parents were of course consoling her.

I wanted to enquire, 'What had happened to her,' but I thought it unwise to interfere. Hence, I pretended, that I'd noticed nothing. For a few minutes, there was silence in the cabin but for the deafening sound of the railway fans and the hissing sound of the engine. The young girl was now leaning on her mum, who was, in turn, stroking her cheeks gently. 'She must be really sick,' I said to myself as she was writhing in pain.

The undivided attention of both parents was on their beloved daughter. They hardly spoke, but I could sense that all the three could emote with each other. What was actually going on between them was difficult to grasp.

In no time, the Brahmaputra Mail rushed into the busy station, and for the first time, I saw the prominent black and bold letters of the name LUMDING, glittering on the yellow board.

The young girl began to weep.

Quickly the gentleman, his wife, and the young man collected her baggage. They all hugged each other and bid a tearful farewell to the young girl. "Don't forget me," she quivered. Until the train pulled out from the station and receded into the distance, the young girl stood waving her hands to her parents.

"Why did your daughter alight in Lumding? What happened to her?" It was a puzzle for me. "Is she unwell?" I asked the gentleman after a pause. With a smile, he replied that the young Zubeni was not their daughter, but a co-traveller from Delhi. They had got close during the travel and exchanged their lives. It was difficult for me to believe that Zubeni was not their daughter. It took some hard time for me to come to grips with the fact.

"Poor Zubeni, a lovely and affectionate girl, she was a daughter to us in the last two days," uttered the lady for the first time.

After a while, the gentleman revealed that Zubeni is a Naga and they were Nepalese. I could then connect the dots of resemblances in their faces. What the two-day train journey had wrought in them was amazing indeed, I thought.

It was time again for tea and snacks. It was my turn to treat all of them. It was fun. The young mother and her child joined us. She was quite talkative.

"Zubeni has gone through a tough time in her life, but she is an indomitable fighter," the young mother stated. The little boy was pulling the cheeks of his mum. He was playing with the locket, clapping his hands and pulling her hair. The mother was, in turn, pampering the child, tickling him and blowing kisses, which he seemed to really enjoy.

Her husband was a contrast, a silent observer all the way. Short in stature, he looked boyish, with no traces of hair on his face. Something in him suggested that he was diffident and out of place.

For the first time, I asked the name of the gentleman. "I am Mr. Chaithri, my wife is Alina." He proudly enlightened me and added that Alina means 'beautiful and bright.' "Your name befits you, Aunty," the young mother remarked. The gentleman's face outshined the face of Alina.

The train gathered momentum and stormed ahead, heading towards Dimapur. My eyes flitted across all my co-travellers. I watched their eyes, compared with one another. It ranged from misty and mysterious to sparking and shimmering. The eye of the little fellow was soulful and angelic. His mom's were hazy. Eyes carry the deepest of emotions. They too often tell a story. Some eyes shine with love, some cold, some bloodshot with anger. Some eyes have the power to heal.

The train was speeding towards Dimapur, which is the commercial centre of Nagaland. On an earlier occasion, during Christmas Eve, we were on our way to Kohima, through Dimapur. Kohima was lit with stars. It was a beautiful sight. Dimapur lies near the border of Assam along the banks of the Dhansiri River.

"It's next, our turn," whined the young mother and kissed her child. She held him tightly to her breasts and wouldn't release him. "Oh! How I love this little cherub. Sir, he is my golden baby," said the mother. "We all jelled well together," remarked Mr. Chaithri. Alina fondled the chubby pink cheeks of the boy. He was like a prince, captivating with his blue and curious eyes. I couldn't take my eyes off him.

Another spate of kisses from his mom…

“What is your name? And where are you heading to?” I asked her.

“Sir, I am Dishru,” she replied, “We are from North Cachar Hills and we are Dimasa. My husband is Donham.”

I recounted to her my adventurous journey to Hafflong, during an ethnic clash between two groups. I described to Dishru the winding roads, the beautiful hills, the gorgeous valleys, the scenic landscape, and the majestic mountains that made my trip an unforgettable one. Dishru had deaf ears to my words of praise, she was engrossed with her child. But I thought that a visit to this one-and-only hill station in Assam makes you feel nostalgic.

While my vivid memories pedalled me into these serene hills, a pall of gloom had abruptly enveloped Dishru, otherwise cheerful in her disposition. I couldn’t figure out what was brewing in the mind of Dishru. Donham sat watching his wife with no reactions.

The train was slowing down….

“We hardly felt the boredom of this arduous journey,” quipped Mrs Alina. “All good things have to come to an end,” added Mr. Chaithri.

Donham rose to collect the baggage.

Winking at me with a teary eye, Dishru whispered, “Sir, I wish, I could flick away this child.”

Startled, I questioned, “Don’t tell me, he is not your child.”

The boy was resting his cheeks on the cheeks of Dishru. It was a beautiful sight. "Sir, his parents are happily asleep in the next cabin." "For the last two days, he has never parted from me. I never knew I would fall so badly in love with Atinga, this Manipuri child. We hardly spoke, but one couldn't have loved better." Before I could digest this unpalatable truth, a young lady, like a snow-clad hill, showed up in the cabin. Spotless, with a beauteous smile, stretched her hand to receive her child, but the little boy turned his eyes away and held Dishru like an ivy creeper. A little war broke in the cabin before Atinga could be extricated.

All of us joined in assisting the Dimasa couple with their baggage. The train halted in Dimapur. Dishru soon appeared through the window from the platform to steal her last glimpses of the treasure that was fully hers for the last two days. The sealed tinted glasses came in as a barrier between the sobbing Atinga and the wailing Dishru. She looked hopeless and miserable. Her tears made a trail on the dust deposits of the window, with her hungry eyes transfixed on Atinga.

In a few minutes, the whistle was blown by the guard. The wheels began their movement. How we hated the whistle, and how much more Dishru and Atinga would've hated them.

There was silence in the cabin for a while… Atinga's father had joined us in the cabin. Little Atinga was still sobbing with his mum doing her bit to pacify him.

What was going on in his little heart, none can understand.

We had a few friendly exchanges with the Manipuri family. The benevolent Mr. Chaithri ordered another cup of tea. Each cup brought us closer.

The Manipuri gentleman asked me, "Have you been to Manipur?" I narrated my travel to Moreh, the commercial hub and border town located on the India–Myanmar border. I told him how I was taken by surprise to listen to Tamil film numbers played out in the town of Moreh. We discussed the cultural diversity and the surreal experience it offers to the travellers, amidst its exquisite beauty of nature.

The train chugged away leaping towards its final destination.

Atinga was under a spell of a tranquil sleep in the arms of his mum. His face was awash with a fragrant innocence and a cute rainbow smile flitted on his lips. For a moment, my thoughts raced after Dishru, what would she be up to? Perhaps she was in a frantic search of motherhood, or pining for pure love.

"What a beautiful camaraderie! What a well-knit plot!" I pondered to myself. A Dimasa couple, a Manipuri family with their cherubic son, a young Naga girl, a Nepali couple, with a south Indian watching the drama unfold in a small cabin of a train in a remote corner of North Eastern India, an ever-enchanting land.

The human heart has no barriers.

“*Their* [goats] *characteristics are calm, and so when you are around them it’s hard to have anxiety or stress because you seem to take on that energy of calmness.*”

– Lainey Morse

Goat Therapist

Farooq's Goat

Evening tea time with Sunny, Serofina, and Noel was special and remarkable in Chikkamagaluru. They kept an open home and Sam and I had the pleasure of joining them on several occasions.

Yesterday's evening was one such memorable and fulfilling one. A neatly trimmed garden adorned the entrance of their home and offered a splendid ambience. The crispy, yummy cutlets rolled out by Serofina were incredibly mouth-watery. Her signature lemon tea, a brand by itself, added a special flavour and taste. Noel's savoury smiles combined with his innocent glances were therapeutic after a hectic day. Sunny always peppered the evening get-together with a story. Visiting their home was a three-fold blessing. Yesterday, he shared a true story that happened years ago in Assam. His repertoire includes a large number of factual and gripping stories. This particular one is interestingly, centred around Farooq's goat. It is a touching story that exemplifies from hoof to the heart.

Farooq was a temporary driver in a boarding school. He was youthful, tall, and muscular. He was flashy, trendy, clean-shaven, and sported a neatly trimmed mush, with well-maintained whiskers. He walked about with his nose in the air. Sadly, his appearances betrayed him. He was perceived to be arrogant and cunning, but he wasn't. All the inmates of the campus disliked him for the attitude that he seemed to throw. His body language suggested that he was villainous and crafty, so all in unison developed an aversion for Farooq and distanced themselves. He was alone and lonely.

This story is set in a temporary campus of a boarding school in Nalbari, Assam. The buildings were dilapidated and the campus was located in a serene environment, with sylvan surroundings. The vast stretches of bristling paddy fields, areca trees, and rich lush greenery added a certain delight.

Life in a boarding school has its challenges. The boundary walls stare at the children. The world outside always seems greener and alluring. Children get bogged down when their freedom is curtailed. Homesickness sometimes keeps gnawing their minds. But that's how life moves on in a boarding school.

Farooq one day brought a goat-kid inside the campus. He did this bereft of official permission. Brown and white in colour, he was a cute little thing with an expressive face, odd eyes, and facial hair. He was allowed to freely loiter on the campus. Even the campus dogs tolerated the newcomer and never perceived this intruder as a threat. Children took an immediate liking for the new pet on the campus. But the elders disliked him. They gossiped about the arrogance of Farooq and his audacity to bring a goat-kid inside the school campus. Their dislike for Farooq spilt over to his pet. They shooed him away.

Farooq's goat had an inquisitive nature. It was evident in his constant drive to explore and investigate anything unfamiliar on the campus. Within a few days, Farooq's goat did not leave any stone unturned on the campus. He became familiar with every corner, meandering and wandering with free access. He was still a kid, with a rectangular pupil that allowed him to see a huge range of the surroundings. His bleat was quite distinct and his calls were unique. He hopped around the campus and was friendly. He did not eat everything he found, he picked a few things and foraged here and there. Farooq's goat browsed anything he found edible, but never grazed like cattle and sheep. He was fond of browsing on the tips of woody shrubs, trees, and small bushes. He preferred to eat leaves, overgrown weeds, and baby trees. Sometimes, he used to climb the top of trees on the campus and had all the signs of soon turning out to be an exceptionally strong billy-goat. The tender bounces of the kid, his cute looks and his claim on everyone on the campus slowly gained acceptance and soon emerged as the official pet of the school.

He played with the children during the games period and was there in the morning assembly, for all the cultural shows, and CCA competitions. The presence of this pet enthused the children. They caressed him and called him by different names: *Junuka*, *Lola*, *Milo*, and *Moina*. Boys and girls fed him, awaited him, and connected with him day by day. He grew extraordinarily playful, sportive, and adventuresome.

When Farooq's goat walked up to the children and started to snuggle, climb up their laps, or gaze at them, it used to make the child feel special. The calm demeanour of this pet was helpful. When he chewed his cud, it was akin to a meditative state that was soothing and relaxing to watch. He was able to differentiate between happy and unhappy faces. He could discern the moods of children and touch them individually.

One day, Biplab, a little boy fractured his hand at play. Unable to bear the pain, he cried profusely. Farooq's goat followed little Biplab as he was carried to the medical room and sat silently, intently watching him and emoting with him in his distress. There are numerous such instances when Farooq's goat facilitated quick relief to the children when they were in pain. The fact that he connected with all the children equally, emoted with them, played with them, being present with them as a companion, endeared him to all the children. They cherished his presence as much as they celebrated him.

During parents' visits, apples, bananas, and other fruits and eatables were brought to him. Children who were in distress, prone to homesickness, and loneliness, sought succour from this loving animal. When any child was sent home, he was there to accompany them to the Main Gate to see them off. He also welcomed the children who were arriving back to the school. Farooq's goat generated a happy feeling, camaraderie, and a sense of belonging that pervaded the campus.

Even the elders and teachers found that engaging with Farooq's goat, petting or cuddling him, could visibly reduce stress and pave the way for overall wellness. The entertaining nature of Farooq's goat and its playfulness could prod children out of their shells and lift their spirits.

Goats are usually herd animals and they are happier when they are a part of the flock. A goat in solitude is a lonely goat, but Farooq's goat never for a minute appeared so. The kid grew in size and stature. When the children left for vacation, they missed their pet and obviously, he equally missed the children too. It was a doleful sight to witness the animal dragging itself on the campus. Its eyes reflected the sadness within. When it bleated, there was a strong strain of melancholy, unlike the usual bleats that reverberated with a happy note. The students in the school became its whole world. He quietly touched the lives of the inmates with his distinct bleats and his gestures filled with warmth.

One day, there was a pick and speak competition and the students spoke on various topics. Incidentally, one of the topics was "Farooq's Goat." A boy zealously began to articulate his thoughts and feelings amidst thunderous applause. The boy was expounding on the emotional attachment of all the students to this beautiful creature. To everyone's amazement, Farooq's goat quickly hopped to the stage and stood beside the speaker. The audience roared in excitement and rose to give a standing ovation to this unusually astounding gesture. There were outbursts of slogans and celebrations, and it turned out to be a festive occasion for the entire school community. Farooq's goat stood there composed acknowledging the peans and praises like a celebrity in style. This became a red-letter day on the campus. Whenever the students joined for a reunion, long after they left the school, they exuberantly recounted this incident with each other.

Surprisingly, all the staff members by now warmed up towards Farooq.

Months passed and the years rolled. Farooq's goat had now grown into a full adult. Tufts of hair hung under its chin like a beard and wattles swelled around the throat. Farooq's goat as a mature adult could look into the eyes of all the children on campus, understand their body language, and distinguish between their sad and happy expressions.

During monsoon, while children loved to play in the rain, he would run to the nearest shelter, often arriving before the first drops of drizzle. He was found to have an aversion to mud and puddles.

Farooq's goat was regularly featured in pictures, cartoons, paintings, journals, scrapbooks, projects, and poems in the school by the children. A caprine on the campus turned around many things positively.

One day, a regular driver joined the school, and Farooq was relieved of his duties. There was no official send-off organized, but as Farooq stood with his goat to leave the campus once-for-all, the entire school thronged and bade a tearful farewell to their beloved pet who was stoutly reluctant to leave his beautiful home and large family. The hour of separation caused a tremor in the hearts and minds of the campus dwellers. As Kahlil Gibran has rightly stated,

> "*And ever has it been*
>
> *Known that love knows*
>
> *Not its own depth until*
>
> *The hour of separation.*"

It took a while for the community, especially the children, to come to terms with the harsh reality of Farooq's goat's absence. The vacuum was acutely felt daily in each of their lives, but life has to go on.

"The comfort of having a friend may be taken away, but not that of having had one."

– Seneca

A Lily of a Day

It is been more than a decade-and-a-half since he died, but still, I feel he is somewhere around. I can hear him strutting the guitar, watch him in deep reverie, or on a way side shop in the Nilgiris relishing the spicy bajji or samosa to his heart's content, with a steaming cup of tea in his hand.

Where did I first meet him? I cannot recollect, but I've always known him since childhood. He is among the few men I still admire. There was a genuineness about him that is irrefutable. As an ardent disciple of Christ, he followed his Master with unswerving faith and dogged faithfulness. He was versatile and could easily play the guitar, write devotional lyrics, compose music, and pipe songs. Ravi Kumar was a gifted teacher, preacher, and translator. His expositions on Moses, the patriarch, and his sessions on Hudson Taylor in Masinagudi Quiet Corner years ago still ring in my mind.

He was an original thinker and would take a stand on almost every issue. He is not someone who would be swayed by every wind that blew around him. He was a practitioner of his faith and demonstrated that "our faith, and our beliefs, should affect our lives and transform it."

Once he took in a stranger to his home, who was a convict and a drug addict just released from prison. He persuaded Sheeba, his young wife, with a little child, to join him in extending hospitality to him. Sheeba was aghast, with a stranger right in her home. "His bloodshot eyes, dilated pupils, abnormal puffiness, the slurred speech, the sloppy behaviour, the injuries on his hands, were terrifying," observed Sheeba, who thought they were at risk, and rightly so. Ravi Kumar on the other hand, believed he was a human in need and we ought to show him compassion. They hosted him for a few days and he arranged funds for the stranger to be deported safely to his home in the Andamans.

On another occasion, he provided accommodation and food for a couple who had eloped to the Nilgiris. They were penniless and hungry. He paid their bills. He has funded many folks' higher education from his scant resources. These are a few samples of the numerous such incidents that vouch for his generosity and compassion. Being a good Samaritan at heart, he was never once proud, boastful, or haughty. He cultivated the passion to be like his Master, in his words, thoughts, and deeds. He was altruistic in his relationships and dealings. Short-statured, curly-haired, dark in complexion, befittingly dressed, with shoes well-polished, he had a charm that can be only his. He spoke less, promised less but delivered more.

Even decades after his demise, when I ponder about him, he appears to me with the same affable smile, friendly overtures, and a gentleness that is binding. He ambled with his military green jerkin and sometimes with his favourite brown sweater.

In one of his sermons, he stated, "When God wants to measure a man, he never puts his tape around his head, but he puts it around his heart."

When he was working for some time in Tiruchendur, in the Tamil Nadu Tourist Department, I received a New Year Card from him, on which he had handwritten, "Our relationship with God must not be based on a storage plan, but on contact plan." He was not mystical or religious but had a spiritual orientation. He never adhered to any form of rituals but had a living relationship with his Heavenly Father.

He was a doting father and a wonderful husband. He spent adequate time with his family and took both Debby and Danny along for long walks. He often played football with Danny, his little son.

Although he was spiritually inclined, he had a unique sense of humour and wit. He could imitate folks with astounding accuracy without hurting them. While his jokes threw his listeners to peals of laughter, he could maintain his composure. Ravi Kumar had a craze for watching street squabbles. He would wait, take time, and observe keenly. Later on, watching him imitate and act out every gesture and movement of folks in the street fight would be an enthralling experience.

My friend was a raconteur par excellence. He narrated anecdotes with a skilfulness that was amazingly humorous.

One such incident is recounted here. A foreign friend of his once invited him for dinner outside. Despite his reluctance, he was coaxed into accepting the invitation. They went to 'Iranis', a restaurant in Ooty town. They chatted over sumptuous dinner and had a whale of a time. Interestingly, after dinner, the foreigner demanded a separate bill from the waiter for both of them. He quickly settled his bill, shoved Ravi Kumar's bill in his hands, and hurried off on his way. Ravi Kumar stood dumbfounded and had to face embarrassing moments without a single penny in his pocket. When he narrated this incident, we could not but laugh, despite our deep sympathies for him. He with his brilliant, narrative style, tone, and tenor, could transform something serious and tragic into a humorous thing.

He visited me twice when I was in Chennai. We had a stroll inside the salubrious, sylvan, and sprawling campus of Madras Christian College. He was deeply impressed with the green cover on the campus, the scrub jungle, and a plethora of flora and fauna. Fortunately, both of us sighted a herd of deer moving around in the scrub jungle. We went to the cricket pavilion, sat there for a long time and enjoyed the breeze. We couldn't talk much, but to spend time with a person who meant a lot to me was fulfilling. As a pluviophile, he enjoyed the drizzle as we walked back to our room.

He was more of an avid listener, thinker, and keen observer. He knew the art of remaining silent when it was not required of him to speak. His studied silence was mature, decisive, and discreet.

On another occasion, we had been to the Marina beach together one evening. We sat on the long stretch of golden sand that overlooks the Bay of Bengal, with spectacular blue-green water lapping the shore. We sat together for what seemed like hours, lost to the magnificent vastness of the sea. Seagulls were soaring and swooping. The mounting waves were rolling and crashing on the shore. The harmonious music of the waves was soothing to the ears.

I saw him absorbed, with his eyes closed in a meditative mood. I heard him humming quietly the famous hymn, 'O Lord my God, when I in awesome wonder.' He was in an act of adoration and prayer. He had attributed the beauty of the ocean to the Creator. Then he gently observed that the boundless ocean is a microcosm of what eternity is, timeless, boundless, magnificent, mysterious. I realized that he had a foretaste, a small glimpse of eternity in those few minutes, but little did I guess that he would soon be embracing it.

It was already dark and the sky was spangled with stars. He wanted to lay hands on the seafood that was available in the eateries at the beach. He relished the lobster bit by bit, which was a real treat to watch. I wouldn't label his craving for food as opsomania, but certainly, he had a craving and enthusiasm for certain foods.

Once, we had dismounted the Doddabetta Peak together, in the evening chill of the Nilgiris, and headed to the Shinkows to warm ourselves with the delicious Chinese soup. As we were gliding down, from the four-road junction, a poor villager was walking before us. Ravi Kumar picked up a conversation, '*Periavare.*' He conversed with him in this typical village style using the local slang. That is how he connected with the commoners. At the end of the journey, in Charring Cross, he tipped the villager and asked him to have tea.

The last time I fondly remember having a great time with him was the boating we together had in Pykara Lake. We had the entire lake to ourselves. It was late in the evening and in the chill, we stayed afloat, only the two of us, in the crystal waters of the Pykara Lake. He was rowing the boat, while I was enjoying the ride. He loved adventure, but he wanted to make the moment special for me.

Life was going well for him. Towards the end of his life, he shared with me that he was concerned about the significance of families. During one of the summer vacations, when I was in Ooty, we had a special evening arranged for all the young families of our friends' circle. He was the brainchild.

When news broke out that he was diagnosed with terminal cancer, I was there to visit him at CMC Vellore. Mr. Oswald Prabhu, another common friend of ours, was also there. We spent time with him and prayed with him. The parting was painful. We hugged each other. His body, I could feel, was frail, but his spirit was strong, and the chords of love and friendship bound us together. He was composed but I couldn't control myself. I broke down. Somehow both of us knew that this is going to be the final farewell. After a few days, he passed away.

He has left behind precious and exceedingly beautiful memories, unanswered questions, but a legacy of faith, along with a vacuum that he alone can fill. Many of us were shaken by his death, and cannot come to terms with it even today.

He gave an extraordinary insight into the evanescent life here on earth and investing in eternity. I get to dream even today of boating in the Pykara Lake, only the two of us, mounting and dismounting the Doddabetta Peak, and strolling in the exotic spots in the Nilgiris.

I sit on this side of the sea and curiously await him to smile, yonder from the other side of the beautiful shore. The eternity that he so vehemently believed had enwrapped him and he embraced it forever.

He is a pretty lily of a day, a flower of ephemeral light, an emblem of humility, gentle and mild. In Ben Johnson's words,

"A lily of a day,

Is fairer far in May,

Although it fall and die that night

It was a plant and flower of light."

www.ingramcontent.com/pod-product-compliance
Lightning Source LLC
La Vergne TN
LVHW041216150826
845673LV00001B/426

* 9 7 9 8 8 9 0 6 6 9 3 9 1 *